# Burdens of Blood

*Legend of the Dawn Child Book ONE*

## Crystal Matthews

*Dedicated to my husband, Steven, for always supporting me. Special thanks to Danielle, Ashley, and Mariha for being muses along the way.*

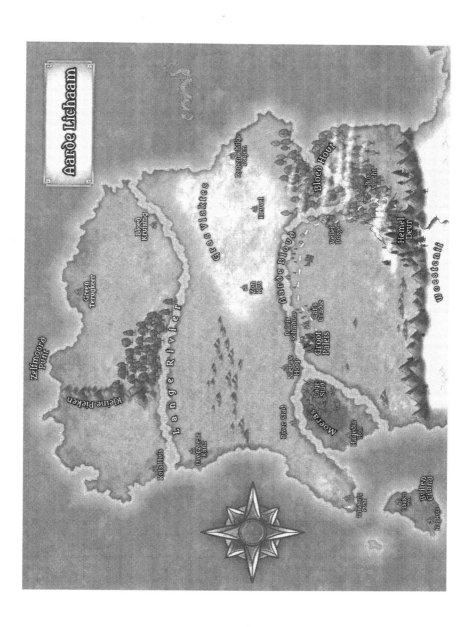

Aarde Lichaam

# *Prologue*

"So you wish to hear a story," one of the tall strangers said quietly. "I suppose you want to hear a tale of one of our adventures?"

The small crowd of children nodded while giggling in agreement. It was not often an outsider passing through the small village stopped long enough to talk with them. These particular travelers were more exciting than most, though not one child could tell you why. The two men were the same height and build; they both had one green eye and one blue. They shared the same smile, and even their dirty riding clothes were identical.

"There are many good ones we've come across in our wanderings … yet, we know a tale that is better than any story we have experienced ourselves." While the first man spoke, the other twin took the time to meet every child's eye.

A farmer hurried by with a small herd of goats and when the stranger glanced up, he found a petite girl hiding just around the corner of a nearby wagon. She was not more than seven winters, yet her eyes shone with memories much older.

"Do you, my dear, wish to hear our tale?"

"Not her!" one of the young boys said. "She's weird."

The quiet stranger studied the cowering girl again. There was nothing out of the ordinary about her; she was small for her age, with scraggly brown hair, and her eyes were a dull blue, almost grey. She held a small chick in the crook of her arm. He motioned for her to sit next to him and she hesitated only for an instant.

"Now then…" the first brother said. "This story is one you will probably never hear again. If you do, it will be spoken in hushed voices late at night." He glanced around to make sure they had all of the children's attention.

"There once was a mighty kingdom, one much darker than where we live now," the other brother continued. "This kingdom was ruled by a mighty king who followed old traditions and praised even older gods. He was a generous man, making sure his wealth was used toward his subjects. He ensured that none of his people suffered from cold or hunger. The people loved him for this, and he loved them all in return." The brother's smile was wistful.

"Well, this king was not only blessed with prosperous lands, he was also blessed with twelve sons and one daughter. Now, the king loved all of his sons equally and never failed to give in to their every desire. His love for his sons was only matched by the scorn for his daughter. You see, his wife, the queen, was taken from this world and delivered through the gates of the Underworld after she'd given birth to the girl. The king had never forgiven his daughter for this," the first man explained.

The small girl next to the twins quietly whimpered in sympathy, squeezing the chick closer. The man smiled down at her and continued.

"All of the king's children grew strong and beautiful while the king himself grew old and crippled. His kingdom must have an heir, but which son would he grant the honor of rule? All were spoiled, greedy, and rotten men. Overindulged and prone to selfish behaviors." The children sneered along with the men.

"He had made them this way with his misguided love. He tried to think of his people; the great king did not want them to suffer. He prayed every night to the gods for guidance, yet received none. He was heartsick at the thought of favoring one son above another, for he loved all twelve equally." The children sat wide-eyed as the men took turns speaking.

"His love for his sons, sadly, was not returned. In the end, it was his daughter that stayed by his bed as he lay dying. His resentment for her grew as he became convinced that she was the reason his great sons did not come. She dutifully ignored his cold words while she wiped the sweat from his brow and changed his linen." The brother shook his head mournfully while the other continued on.

"The king was a faithful servant of the old gods, and his daughter knew they would be angry when her brothers did not visit the dying king. The gods did not sit blind to the people that loved them, and her father had always spread his faith throughout the kingdom. Her brothers' acts would not go unpunished. She knew because the gods had told her themselves, in her sleep."

"The gods were very kind to her, and she listened when they spoke about the future and her place in the world. She listened when they told her about her father needing her now. Most of all, she listened to them when they spoke of the wrongs that had befallen her and how everything would be made right again soon."

"One morning, she found her father limp in his bed. The great king had finally passed the gates of the Underworld to be with his wife forever. In his frail, wrinkled hand, he held a rolled parchment. Looking through a veil of tears, the daughter carefully unrolled it. To her shock, the king had decided who his heir would be. In his final days, he had sketched a map of the kingdom, yet it was not the kingdom she recognized now. The map was split into twelve separate provinces, each one named after one of her brothers. She closed her eyes, overcome with grief. Not only for the loss of her father but also for the fate of her people. The gods had warned her of the disaster that would come when her brothers were in power."

The children sat wide-eyed, completely enthralled by the tale, but none more so than the petite girl. "What happened next?" she asked as the chick crawled onto her shoulder.

"Well, the sons predictably destroyed all that lay in their path. They acted like parasites, leeching the life out of their share of the kingdom. Their greed destroyed crops and starved the people. Anyone who protested would be executed on the spot. The land turned to ash while whole forests were cut down to build palaces. Mountains were mined to sculpt monuments for the brothers. The royal treasury dried up because the brothers did not care about the cost of their habits. They were kings now, and kings answered to no one."

"The people wept to the gods and cried out for justice. The gods listened to all their faithful children, and they knew this horror must end before there was nothing left to save. They gathered together, and it was agreed they would not simply destroy the brothers, but would allow them a chance at redemption. A chance to learn from their mistakes and honor their father like he deserved."

The two men had attracted a small crowd now, a few passersby stopping to hear the story as well.

"After only five years of rule, the brothers gathered to celebrate their own greatness. It would be a spectacular night with feasting, mead, wine, girls, and dancing. The attendees were vile creatures, much like the brothers. Some were personal guards; others were highborn nobles seeking favor. All were rotten inside."

"The only daughter of the former king was not forgotten by her brothers. They had treated her much like their father before them—always keeping her close but never allowing her freedom."

"'Sister,' the kings had called on the day of their celebration, 'bring us wine so we may toast to our greatness!'"

"She hurriedly brought out twelve goblets made of fine gold. They overflowed with rich, almost black wine. The brothers drank deeply and soon they were all too drunk to stand, smiling to themselves as they fell fast asleep."

The man who spoke stumbled as if drunk himself, eventually pretending to fall asleep on his twin's shoulder. The crowd giggled in unison.

"The first brother who awoke was stiff and groggy from the night's activities, not remembering much from the night before. He found he was surrounded by tall trees. He tried to concentrate but could not figure out why there were trees in the middle of this great hall. Confused, he tried to take a step, but did not move.

"'Why can I not move?' he asked out loud.

"'I cannot move either, dear brother,' came a reply.

"The first brother could not find his kinsmen anywhere.

"'Nor I!' came another cry.

"Completely baffled, the first brother to wake called out, 'What kind of trickery is this? Why can I not move, why can I not see my brothers? I demand to know where I am! Guards!'

"It was his sister's voice that answered his cries.

"'I fear, my beloved brothers, that you have drunk bad wine,' she said with a sneer. 'It seems you have all been turned into trees.' Then she began to giggle uncontrollably.

"Not wanting to believe his lowly sister, he called out again. 'Brothers, where are you hiding?' His distress only made her laugh louder.

"'The gods have punished you all for your greedy ways.

They came to me in my dreams, you see, they demanded justice for what you have done to Aarde Lichaam and the people who live here.' She danced in circles as she spoke. 'Do not fear, brothers, the gods are not blind in their hate. You will get a chance to prove yourself true believers again. When ten thousand cycles of the seasons have passed, you must stand before a female descendant of our clan. Only she can decide if you are worthy to rule as men again.' She cackled hysterically.

"'How can we redeem ourselves when we are trees?' they all called at once. She stopped dancing and stared into nothing for a long time.

"Finally, she spoke. 'The gods are not cruel; you may keep your loyal guards and servants to protect and serve you. Good luck, brothers, perhaps we will see each other again.' She gave them one last look, then turned and skipped away. She was finally free of her tormentors and the kingdom would know peace again."

With the story told, the brothers smiled at each other as the excited children ran off to play games and dream of great forests ruled by evil men.

They had found her at last. How pleased the Elders would be.

# Chapter One

"Starlyn, Starlyn." The familiar voice broke through her dreams, but she refused to acknowledge it. She focused again on the dreamy comfort that she was losing grasp of.

"Starlyn, you're already late!"

She moaned softly to herself. The voice would not be ignored and the dream could not be regained. Her eyes responded slowly to her command to open, as if they too were not ready for the day.

When the words of the voice settled into her mind, her eyes popped open immediately. She sat up instantly and stared groggily at her mother in disbelief. The cold in her mother's soft blue eyes told her the truth of things; she was running very late indeed.

Normally, she was the first one up and done with half her chores by now. Quickly, she jumped up from her straw mattress on the floor and scampered to the chest next to it, brushing aside the fat hen which rested on it. It clucked at her annoyingly, but for once she did not care.

Not focusing on her lack of selection, she hastily pulled out a heavy skirt and the cleanest tunic she could find. Both were too big for her, and the worn shoes she slid on her feet were equally too small. She grabbed her hooded cape that hung next to the doorless entry that led to her room and threw it over her shoulders.

She followed on the heels of her mother, squinting in the light that poured through the windows. The sun was well above the horizon. She groaned in dismay; her father would not be happy.

She quickly smoothed down her dark brown hair, wishing she had time to make it a bit more presentable. As she headed toward the front door, her mother handed her two slices of warm, thick bread with honey drizzled on top. She smiled brightly at her mother before kissing her cheek and accepting breakfast.

Finally out the door, she jogged toward the shearing shed in the back of the house and was greeted by the familiar bleating of hungry sheep. She winced; her lateness was the reason their sheep were hungry.

Her father was guiding the cart of wool out of the double doors already. Her mouth went dry. He was never forgiving when it came to the running of their farm. Cramming the rest of her meal into her already full mouth, she took the rope that was tied to the mule from his hands and finished the job that he'd started. Once the mule was secured, she turned to face him.

"I know I don't have to say anything to you," he said, disapproval in his grey eyes. "You've always been harder on yourself than on other people." She grimaced, knowing the truth of his words. She tried hard to make him proud, and it burned her to the core if she disappointed him.

"I don't know what happened, Papa. My dreams don't let me sleep, and then ... I don't know, they don't let me wake up," she countered, honestly noticing how absurd and childish she sounded.

He turned to stare at the house for a time. "Your mother may be able to help you. She used to have strange dreams ... But for now, you're late. It's gonna rain soon judging by those clouds." He nodded toward the building darkness in the sky.

Starlyn understood his meaning and dragged the oiled

canvas from the shed and secured it over the bundles of wool. That should do for a time. Her father nodded again, this time in farewell, as she untied the mule and began down the road to *Groot Paleis*.

It began to rain not long after she had left the safety of her family's small farm. The big drops were falling heavy, and soon the cart of wool was soaked despite the oiled canvas covering it. Her home in *Paleis Schaduw* was only a short distance from *Groot Paleis*, yet in this kind of weather the road was endless. Brushing back her wet hair from her face, Starlyn walked on, knowing the whole time she could've avoided the rain if she had not slept in.

"No point in rushing now, everything's already soaked," she commented to the old mule pulling the cart as it splashed through another puddle. "I'm sure my uncle will love the fact that the wool from last shearing before winter will need to be dried before he can use it."

Her sarcastic tone was hiding her discomfort. Uncle Tomlin would be furious about it being wet. She told herself she would leave out the part about her running late and maybe her visit would be somewhat enjoyable.

As she trudged along the road, a small group of children playing in a nearby mud puddle caught her eye. She smiled longingly at them; how nice it seemed to have friends. She was always alone as a child, never quite good enough to earn the other children's friendship. She never knew why. Bitterness began to creep into her already bad mood. She tried hard not to live in the past, so she brushed off the unwelcome feelings and continued forward.

It seemed almost an eternity before other people were visible on the road. It was the normal traffic she had seen hundreds of times before reaching the outer wall, just much less of it. She'd been very young when she first accompanied her father on this trip despite her mother's protests. She pictured the sunny day when her mother finally consented to the trek after it became apparent the other children wouldn't play with Starlyn. Her mother hated the way the other kids teased her only child and couldn't stand Starlyn being abused any longer.

Her thoughts continued to drift as she recalled the first time her father showed her the city. She let her mind wander further, to the day he asked her to do the trip alone. It was so long ago, but she still envisioned his somber face and her mother's wide eyes when she took the cart out on her own. At the time, it was the greatest adventure in the world, one she had been waiting to have her whole life. She smiled inwardly. The excitement had long faded; it was now just another boring chore.

Her musing was interrupted as she sloshed into a puddle, soaking her foot instantly and bringing her back to the task at hand. The other travelers who were brave and endured the rain looked just as wet and miserable as Starlyn. She shrugged her cloak tighter and walked on.

Soon the walls of *Groot Paleis* were visible in the distance. The first and outermost wall loomed high above her head, the palace spires barely visible behind the cover of low clouds. The dreary weather made the wall look sinister, and Starlyn reminded herself that this wall was built for protection, not for beauty. Knowing this did not prevent her from shuddering as she passed through the gate and under the murder holes.

The line inside the gate was much shorter than usual and the guards were working quickly. Her cart of wool was checked over and marked down on a long list of other goods coming in this way. Her uncle would have to pay taxes on his deliveries just like everyone else. Standing there in the rain, waiting for the guards to work, she found her attention wandering again. She kicked a rock with her toe, wincing when it stung more than she expected.

She glanced around at the long row of barns and warehouses across from the outer wall, forming a wide road. Patrols were walking with their heads down, glancing into dark corners every now and then. What kinds of merchandise filled those structures? Buyers and sellers had begun to stock up for the winter months and these would be full of goods by now.

The officer at her cart finally finished up and handed her a soggy piece of parchment with numbers and the King's seal on it, which she quickly put away in her cape.

"Almost there now," she said determinedly to her mule.

Dodging mud holes, beggars, stray dogs, and merchants was a chore in itself as she traveled the rain-soaked streets heading toward the center of the vast city. The lower levels were always more crowded than the upper ones, and she had learned quickly to put her head down and keep moving in this area. It was never a good idea to draw attention to the fact that she was alone.

It didn't take long for her to reach the more decorative gate marking the boundary between the working class and the well-kept shops and homes of merchants. Unlike the practical design of the outer gate, this one was well adorned with beautiful metalwork dragons that held lanterns in their claws. The guards here were protected from the rain by brightly colored cloth awnings.

The insides of these walls were full of lovely murals, telling stories of hero's tales along a garden path lined with benches. The streets were paved with cobblestones in place of the muddy dirt roads and had gutters running down both sides, allowing water to drain.

Seeing the difference in streets reminded Starlyn how very different the city was compared to her community outside its walls. Her town worked together when something needed to be done and helped families whose goods were not as profitable that year. The villagers may live farther apart, yet they were much closer together than city dwellers.

The blatant separation between classes bothered her; leaving the unfortunate behind in the mud never failed to make her sad. She knew the wrongness of the whole thing, but that didn't matter. This was the way things were.

She tried not to pay attention to the beauty of this area and made her way to the usual alleys she was told to take. If she was found on the clean streets with her cart, she would be fined a large tax that her father or uncle could not afford. On top of that, her uncle would not risk the secret of where he bought his fine wool. He liked to tell his customers that it was imported from faraway lands, leaving out the fact these lands were his brother's farm in *Paleis Schaduw*.

Two rain-soaked hours after entering the city, Starlyn finally pulled up behind her uncle's textile shop. She was promptly greeted by her very round and very short, red-faced Uncle Tomlin stumbling down the back stairs. He was closely followed by an assortment of hired help. As usual, he was dressed almost foolishly foppish, in a short black satin jacket that only accented his wide belt line. The fine silk shirt he wore was a very modern shade of orange, and his too-tight breeches looked as if they would burst any minute.

"Dear girl, you look just like the drowned rat I found in the rain barrel this morning. I guess it would be too much to hope that my wool was dry, am I right?" he huffed at her, clearly out of breath from his short walk. Starlyn smiled coldly from under her inadequate threadbare hood. She had expected this, after all.

The paid men and women hustled to and fro trying to get the mule, cart of wool, and themselves into a dry environment. At this moment, her friend the mule was being stubborn again. *Better them than me.*

"So, child, was it a good trip? No mishaps, I suspect?"

Uncle Tomlin asked while Starlyn put her hooded cape on a nail by the kitchen fire.

"Of course it was," she replied smugly. "I just love a good frolic in the rain." Her uncle either didn't notice the sarcasm or decided to ignore it.

He busied himself directing the women in the kitchen to get tea and biscuits ready as soon as it was convenient. Starlyn followed her uncle through the kitchen into the familiar room and table in the back of the store to wait for her tea. To her disappointment, not only was the tea watery, but her uncle took the time to try and be polite by making conversation. She was too cold and tired to deal with any of his pleasantries. This resulted in an annoying nagging sensation as he buzzed questions in her ear.

She'd just begun to find herself getting dry and actually tuning out her uncle when the little silver bells above the shop door tinkled joyfully. Uncle Tomlin was up in a flash—for a round little man, he sure moved fast when money was at stake. As she tried to finish her tea in order to return home, he greeted the customer but his tone was more subdued than normal. Another man's voice responded low and muffled, making it impossible to tell what he had said. It was apparent by her uncle's tone that he was uncomfortable. This made Starlyn beyond curious. She set down her tea and peeked out the door to see the nature of this customer.

He was at least a head and a half taller than herself, which meant compared to her uncle the man was like a giant. He was lean with broad shoulders and wore a black cape with the hood over his head. As he spoke, he took a step forward, revealing more of himself. He wore black leather gloves and boots that laced up to his knees. He moved with a subtle grace that was disarming—until you realized he wore two swords, one at his hip and a larger one on his back. Starlyn's gaze locked on to the sword at his back, and a chill washed over her. This man was dangerous.

He turned his head, giving the room a quick review, and Starlyn sucked in a breath. The man wore a featureless white mask that hid his face completely. The whole outfit succeeded in covering every inch of his body except for his eyes. That was the most shocking thing about the man; it was not the strange attire or demeanor. It was his eyes. They were a brilliant green, shining bright in contrast to the stoic mask. One word immediately came to mind: Guardian. As shocking as it was, this man was a Guardian.

Growing up, she'd heard many stories about these people. Guardians were a popular topic among travelers, and living next to a well-traveled road like she did, there were always rumors. They were minions of what some called the Elders and others called gods. Some spoke of them as if they were myths, but now she understood why they were feared throughout the land. You could see death in this man's eyes.

Folks whispered about people and businesses that supported the old ways, but it was not a popular thing to do these days. Followers were regarded as fanatics by the current King. His Highborn made sure the old traditions were just that, old.

Forgetting herself, she stepped into the doorway, and the stranger's mysterious eyes found hers immediately. Noticing the change in his patron, her uncle turned around and followed the gaze of the stranger. His eyes grew large and his jaw went slack, as he obviously wasn't expecting Starlyn's entrance. He acted as if she had seen something she wasn't supposed to.

"Come now, girl, shoo, I don't need your assistance right now." Starlyn barely heard a single word her uncle had said.

The man in the mask gently moved Tomlin to one side and bowed, his eyes never leaving hers.

"There is no reason to hide her." He spoke low and smooth, as if he wasn't wearing a mask at all. "I am what is known in the old tongue as *De Beschermer*. I am in service to *De Oudsten*."

Starlyn was frozen, captivated by those green eyes. She never imagined being so close to an actual Guardian, let alone meeting one in her family's shop. Pride fanned through her chest suddenly. Her uncle cleared his throat and succeeded in regaining the Guardian's attention.

Her uncle regained his confidence rather quickly. "A fine cape you say, heavy enough for winter travel. An easy enough task, and one I have done many times. What size shall the second one be?"

The stranger eyed her up and down, making her suddenly uncomfortable.

"The size of this woman," the man said. "Also, a heavy riding skirt and a warm tunic. I understand how difficult it is to get a promissory note from my, how should I put it … employers, cashed so I will do this myself. I need them ready by tomorrow." It was clear the Guardian already knew her uncle would meet his unreasonable requirements.

"You are very kind, good sir, for understanding the lack of banker integrity these days. Never fear, tell the Elders I am still their man." Her uncle bowed low to the ground, looking very awkward.

The Guardian turned and bowed again to Starlyn, touching her hand to where his mouth would have been if not covered by the mask. The little bells above the door had stopped singing by the time she realized he was gone, and Uncle Tomlin had a red-faced scowl on again. She blushed brightly in return.

"Well, my brother will have to understand that you have to stay here tonight. Foolish girl. I must use you for my mannequin." Her father would not be angry. He loved his brother dearly and always said family came first. Despite not exactly liking her uncle, she would do anything he asked of her. It was just the way their family was.

She glanced at the door, still not hearing anything her uncle was saying. Excitement washed over her. She would see the Guardian again.

# Chapter Two

The Guardian had taken only a few steps out of the tailor shop before he was sure he was being followed. He recognized the patterns easily enough, even through the dull patter of rain. It was not an amateur that gave chase; whoever it was would not have been detected by most men. Turning a corner, he did not bother to cover his path. After all, he was *De Beschermer*, a Guardian of the Elite. The Elders may not be popular, but they were still feared. He smoothly rounded the next building and waited patiently with his back to the wall. It was dangerous to keep this game going for too long and he would not tolerate a spy tailing him—his mission was too important.

He only waited a moment before stepping back into the street while pulling the curved knife from behind his belt, a motion that was second nature to him. If he aimed for the throat, it would be over quick and clean, just the way he preferred.

The man sucked in a breath, startled by his own mistake. The Guardian was seconds away from hitting his mark when he saw a blur of a staff coming from behind him. How had he missed the second man? He should have known there was more than one.

Reacting instinctively, he changed course just in time to block the blow with his forearm. The strike flung the knife from his hands. With the opposite hand, he jerked the staff from the attacker's grasp. Using his newly acquired weapon, he slammed both men against the nearby building, where they were pinned down by the staff pressing hard on their necks. It was then he recognized the nature of his followers and eased up on the pressure he applied.

"I assumed that *De Zoekers* would use more caution when following one of their own," the Guardian said with no apparent malice. It would take much more than a pair of Seekers to rattle his nerves.

"It is you that should be the Seeker, friend," the first one said in a slightly choked voice, unsurprised at their defeat.

"You have found your mark all by yourself," the second one finished, breathing heavily.

The Guardian released them and returned the staff to its owner, who quickly retracted it with an unseen switch. The staff, which was now not much longer than his forearm, was easily put away on his belt.

"Ah … I am Jack-obee," the first said.

"And I am Jack-obide," the second man again finished.

"We brothers bow to you, sir, and we are here to report."

They bowed in unison and the Guardian found himself curious about the origin of the two men before him. Seekers always traveled in pairs, but it was rare to meet brothers. Even more strange, they were twins, perfectly matching each other in tone and in movement. No wonder he never perceived the second one following him.

"Then you may report," he responded respectfully in return.

They both glanced to each other and spoke as one. "You have already found what you seek." They nodded in agreement.

"The girl you have come to escort to *Hemel Deur* is in the shop you just left," Jack-obee explained.

"Her name is Starlyn DeTousan and she is the tailor's

niece," finished Jack-obide.

An image of the girl flashed in the Guardian's mind. His eyebrows lifted as he reflected on what fate had given him. She was young, and her dark brown hair had been limp from the rain. Her oversized clothes were worn down and plain. Her eyes were sad and grayish blue.

Overall, she was nothing out of the ordinary. He never would've guessed she was the one he sought—which was good. If he couldn't outwardly see her importance, then others would easily overlook her as well. Focusing his attention back on his strange companions, he scoffed. They were grinning from ear to ear.

"I need both of you to deliver the letter to her parents." He put up his hand, cutting off all protest that may or may not come forth. "You take the lead in finding the safest route back to *Tran Aan Hemel*, then *Hemel Deur*. It is imperative we succeed in getting the girl back safely. She is everyone's responsibility now, priority one."

The twins nodded in unison.

"I have one more task to complete before I may leave. Tomorrow I will retrieve the girl from her uncle and we'll leave by the South Gate. I'll expect you two with a full report of the surrounding area shortly after we reach Cat's Cradle."

They both bowed again before responding, "By the command of the Elders."

The Guardian tilted his head in return. There was much to do before dawn tomorrow, but first he had a certain dirty banker to visit. He reached into his cape and handed over one of the sealed parchments he had carried for weeks now.

Without another word, he turned and headed for the street the locals called the Road to Servitude. It was filled with the greedier of professions that would eventually drain your pockets until you had to work off your debt. Bankers and pickpockets alike clustered themselves into this one foul street, waiting for their next victim.

The Guardian was looking for one particular nasty little man known only as Pelf. He had been a good man once, and had exclusively worked for the Elders. He recently strayed from the following and had begun to give out loans to men that could not get them anywhere else. Loans that were impossible to pay off. The transactions of men were not his concern, however; he was here for a purpose.

The Guardian came to an alley located between two identical nondescript buildings. At the end of the alley was a solitary door, which he had stood in front of many times before. He knocked loudly, then when nothing happened, he turned the handle and found that the door was barred from the inside. Maybe Pelf had heard he was in town already. He gave one good kick, which knocked the door completely off its hinges. The Guardian stepped through the recently opened door and dodged the heavy book that was thrown from a dark corner of the musty room.

"Pelf, that was not very polite. I thought you would've learned your place by now," he commented coolly while he walked to the desk in the corner of the dim room.

Grabbing one side, he easily flipped the desk out of his way, revealing a shivering and sickly thin man beneath.

"I have been ordered to speak with you," he said after jerking the puny man up and tossing him against the far wall. "You have broken your agreement. *De Oudsten* have condemned your soul for this digression, do you understand?"

The feeble man jumped up from where he'd crumpled to the ground and snatched up a sword hanging on the wall behind him.

"You bastard! Your Elders have no power over me. I have a new mistress now!" he hissed, and then charged full speed toward him.

The Guardian drew the blade strapped to his back, and then time stood still. The air shimmered slightly in a wave from the sword as the entire room frosted over. Despite the overpowering blue light which shone from the blade, Pelf did not slow his charge. With every step, his breath puffed out a white cloud in the frosty room. It was the Guardian's blade that struck first, piercing the heart of the traitor. Pelf's eyes went wide and distant, then they slowly began to cloud over with frost.

He dislodged Pelf's frozen body from his blade and quickly put it away. He took a step for the door and fell to one knee. Eyes rolling back into his head, he shuddered while gritting his teeth at the familiar sensation of ecstasy. He took deep breaths until the wave of pleasure was over and when his eyes opened, he found himself on his knees, facing the exit.

Acting as if nothing had happened, he casually brushed off his leather pants and walked to the open door. Just before stepping over the threshold, he flipped a single gold coin over his shoulder and did not bother to see where it landed.

He was not told the reason Pelf was condemned to die, and he did not care. The only thing that mattered was the orders he was given. That was why he had the honor of wearing all black, and that was why he'd been chosen to escort the girl. He was always loyal. The only thing left was to collect the girl. He hoped she didn't fight him too much, as he had been ordered to bring her back—even if it meant in chains.

# Chapter Three

The informant was right about one thing: Pelf was most certainly deceased. The condition of the body, however, was out of the ordinary. The Necromancer had instructed his informant to preserve the body as best as possible, but this was a little too far. How the man had accomplished freezing the corpse solid was a different subject altogether, and one he didn't have time to dwell on.

His informant had done well when he quickly reported the Guardian's attack and execution of Pelf. He might be a drunk, but he was good at keeping an eye on things for him.

The Necromancer drew a small nub of soft red stone from his belt pouch and sketched a line around the corpse of the late Pelf, and then a matching one for himself. He wrote the symbols carefully on the outside of both circles to create the marker beacons. If these weren't done correctly, it would be difficult to find his way home.

Satisfied with his work, he sat cross-legged in his own circle and slowly began to relax every muscle in his body, breath by breath. After some time, he opened his eyes. When his vision focused, he saw he was no longer in the room his body was left in. There was only a low hum coming from where he'd set the beacons. He smiled to himself. How long had he trained in order to accomplish a connection to this world? He glanced around, making sure he was alone, then he closed his eyes again and concentrated on the vision of the first gate.

He was standing in front of what appeared to be a thick wall of mist. He always loved this gate. The walls were wispy, the souls waiting to pass the next gate slowly coming in and out of view. The souls and creatures residing here were the least dangerous you found in the Underworld.

This being the first gate on the journey through the Underworld meant most here walked around confused, not understanding where or why they came. Sometimes the souls lost in the fog would notice you watching them, but most of the time they couldn't care less. Like all of the gates of hell, this one was relatively easy to pass through, but once you tried to come back, you would find that it was near impossible.

There were, however, a few nastier creatures that stalked this gate, looking for a soul to steal or a way to escape to the world of the flesh. They were not foolish enough to bother with him, though. Most demons tried to avoid the Necromancer.

There were certain demons, though, that waited specifically for his arrival, demons that must be avoided at all costs if he valued his soul. He reminded himself to stay vigilant.

Refocusing on why he was here, he checked his magical alarms for signs of Pelf's soul. He had been paid well to make sure Pelf's soul was not lost in death for long. The Necromancer had set alarms at nearly every gate to tell him when the man's soul had passed through it. The problem was, his alarms had not yet triggered.

This being the very first gate, he assumed the only explanation for his alarms to not have worked would be that Pelf had not passed yet. Maybe somehow the banker was stuck here, just outside the first gate. Yet he found himself completely alone, and it was hard to hide his irritation as he stepped through the first gate.

Though the walls appeared to be mist, crossing the gate was like walking through water, making the limbs sluggish and difficult to move. He ignored the unpleasant sensation and pushed through.

Sighing deeply in frustration, he squatted down on the other side of the gate and pulled out the small wooden flute. Raising it to his lips, he played softly, nothing more than a whisper into the wind. The whisper was only a few bars long, but there was a response almost instantly.

Summoning a greater demon had its own unique pattern. It vibrated the air around him, almost like a heartbeat. But that was impossible; this monster had no heart. Not in the human sense.

His own heart quickened as the creature began to take shape out of the ground itself. Its black form bubbled like tar as it solidified into something more recognizable. The being which grew before him was the worst kind of demon. A violent trickster, it was almost always unpredictable.

This particular greater demon was feared by many others in the Underworld. Despite this, he had no apprehension toward the demon and did not hold back the smile that broke over his face. His relationship with the creature was one of the many reasons he was hunted in the Underworld. Their friendship was strictly forbidden.

The monster had chosen a form which was much like a human, only with sticky, wet black skin. It had no eyes to see from and no apparent mouth to speak, yet spoke it did.

"Trust from the House of Riyaadh, it has been a long time since you've called upon me." The creature bubbled and hissed out the words.

"My good demon, I have lost a soul. Pelf was his name in the world of men. I hoped you perhaps would be willing to assist me in locating it?"

The demon said nothing, only tilted its head to one side as if listening to something. After a few minutes, it shook its head. "You and I both know that I am no *good* demon. I am sorry, but no soul has visited here by that name."

"That's impossible. I have his body with mine now. I guarantee no soul resides there," Trust said, rising from the ground. Too much delay attracted unwanted attention, both here and in the mortal world.

"I cannot help you. Perhaps the soul has found a new vessel to thrive in," the demon finally said.

The creature would not go out of its way to help a human. It did not matter how long he had known him or how many times they had explored Death's Gates together. It was simply a law that could not be broken. This little encounter, like so many others, could be misconstrued as bending that law. Without someone willing to enforce it, though, it would go unnoticed.

"Perhaps ..." He bowed slightly to the creature. "Thank you, my *evil* one. Until next time."

Trust turned toward the misty wall once again.

He was risking much by staying in one spot so long. Dealing with the dangers of the Underworld was only part of the battle. He now had to ponder about what the Mistress would think of this incident. He was not looking forward to facing her if she found out he had lost Pelf's soul.

By the time Trust had opened his eyes in the mortal world, the sun was just beginning to turn the sky grey, threatening to be another rainy day. Stiff legged, he walked to the spot where the informant leaned against the wall. The man reeked of rum and the bottle which lay next to him was empty. Sighing to himself, he kicked the man hard.

"You said a Guardian did this to Pelf," Trust said.

The man, in some shock, nodded in agreement.

"Then where is the coin?"

He visibly paled at the mention of the coin. If it truly was a Guardian that killed Pelf, they would have left a gold coin with a picture of a tree imprinted on it with the body. Everyone knew that the Elders were careful to claim their dead. They made sure it left a lasting impression filled with warning and helped fuel the mystique of the old ways.

The man was shaking now as he reached into his trousers where his coin purse was hidden and withdrew the coin. Trust waved it away, knowing the man needed the gold. All he was looking for was the proof.

He sighed deeply to himself as he turned back to Pelf's body and recalled a bit of information that had caught his attention as it crossed his web of spies earlier. The city guard had stopped and held two men at the North Gate. They considered them suspicious, possibly spies for the Elders. The description of the two made him almost certain they were Seekers. He had listened offhandedly at the time, for a pair of Seekers was not an unusual thing. Yet the Seekers' appearance and this Guardian were not a coincidence. Furthermore, he could not fathom why the Elders would require the help of Seekers to find a man like Pelf, which only meant that they were here for someone else. He didn't have much time left to find out who before the Mistress became aware of Pelf's disappearance.

He whipped back to his hired help so suddenly the man almost fell over.

"Find the Guardian ... *now.*"

# Chapter Four

Starlyn had only been asleep for a second when a loud rap on her door abruptly woke her. She had slept terribly, her mind constantly returning to the memory of the hypnotic effect the Guardian had on her. His eyes were unforgettable, seeing everything at once, maybe even her soul. She smiled to herself, and her face began to flush with heat. It was a feeling she did not understand. Something in the corner of her mind, hiding just out of reach.

The person knocked again. Groaning loudly, she got up and answered the door. To her disappointment, her blurry eyes were greeted by her uncle's very red face, a sight she was becoming accustomed to.

"I will not be delayed by your laziness, Starlyn. You know that I have a reputation to keep," he huffed at her.

Too tired to feel ashamed, she followed her uncle down the stairs, bumping into the wall a few times along the way. Unsurprisingly, the shop workers were ready and waiting, looking fresh as ever.

Hoping to gain some time to wake up, Starlyn glanced around the room until she spotted a silver pot filled with hot coffea. She was grateful her uncle was not only known for clothes but also for his exotic imports. Her favorite being the variety that gave you a buzz. She had almost reached her goal when a very large woman stepped in front of her and unceremoniously pushed her into the little back room to start the work of measuring, poking, and prodding.

It was well into midday when she was finally able to sit down and enjoy her first cup of the coffea. She stared blankly out the window while sipping the hot drink. The day was just as dismal as the one before it. The clouds hung low and dark, threatening to unleash a torrent of water at any minute. Her eyes were weary from tossing all night, and as she stared out at the world, her thoughts began to drift to the Guardian. It was getting late. Was he staying dry? Why did she care if he was dry or not? Her lack of sleep was obvious now and her eyes drooped lazily. Her daydreaming was interrupted by one of the younger seamstresses.

"We need you to try on the finished product now, milady," the shy girl said respectfully.

Smiling, Starlyn followed her into the back room. After some effort at donning the skirt and tunic, she studied herself in the full-length mirror. Clothing was not her specialty, but this was impressive work. The material was thick and comfortable, but at the same time it was soft and warm.

She turned left and right, examining herself. When had she become so grown up? The cut of the tunic with the tie at the waist seemed to accentuate how very adult looking she was. She lifted her dark brown hair off her neck, then ran her fingers through it to untangle some of the knots she had created last night. She must invest in some new clothing. The clothes she had now were not nearly as comfortable as ones created to fit her form, and most definitely did not make her feel this proud.

The shop door sounded, and Starlyn's heart stopped. She listened as her uncle greeted the patron with the kind of respect you would greet the king, which meant the Guardian had returned. Her heart beat wildly and she began to breathe faster. From what? Fear? Excitement? She wasn't sure.

Her uncle called her name, and she took a final deep breath. She would not be a silly little girl any longer and she would not swoon over a man when she had never even seen his face. As she walked into the room, she made sure to look the man directly in the eyes, trying her best to settle her nerves. Her uncle was not pleased by her show of disrespect.

"Starlyn, please turn and let the man see what he is buying."

She blushed before complying with his request

Facing the Guardian again, her newfound composure began to slip away. She smiled brightly, trying to cover up her own red face.

"I am glad to see you are still here," the Guardian said, bowing politely. Uncle Tomlin sucked in a breath of surprise while Starlyn's smile immediately vanished. "You have been summoned to stand before *De Oudsten*, and I have been ordered to escort you to *Hemel Deur*."

Her jaw dropped open as he handed her a sealed parchment with her name neatly printed on the front. Her chest constricted.

"And if I refuse your summons?" she whispered without thinking.

The Guardian's eyes visibly darkened and she flinched instinctively. Before he answered, Uncle Tomlin stepped between them.

"Of course she will go with you, sir. The Elders are still respected by this family. It is a great honor," Tomlin stated, bowing low to the ground.

Regaining some confidence, Starlyn pushed her uncle to one side. She suppressed the sudden feeling of panic before speaking. "I need to know what the summons is for or I'm not agreeing to anything ... And what about my papa? I can't just leave him."

The Guardian never blinked once while she was talking, and he now took a moment to study her better.

"It is not my place to know why you were summoned, only that I have been assigned as your *Beschermer*. As for your parents, they have already been informed. I will return in one hour. Pack anything you might want to bring, it will be a long journey." He bowed his head to her, then to Tomlin, before he turned for the door.

"I can't leave without saying goodbye—I'm all they have." She grimaced, trying to not sound like a begging child. She turned to her uncle and pleaded, "They need me now more than ever on the farm. With winter coming, I must be there to help ready the flock."

He smiled sadly. "Now, my dear girl, this truly is a great honor. You may not know it now, but our family have been loyal followers of the Elders for a long time and to finally be summoned is highly desirable. Just think of your farm's reputation once it is learned the only child of the DeTousan family has been summoned."

She knew deep down everything he said was true, but her mouth had gone dry. She had always wanted to travel, but not like this—not without any explanation. Her mother would be so proud of her, though. It could double their business if they were known to be favored by the Elders.

The Guardian was silent for a long moment.

"I will give you one day. You may return home to say your goodbyes, but you will be here at this time tomorrow. Understood?"

A rush of relief washed through her.

"If you try to leave, I will find you. It would be much easier for everyone if you do not run."

He reached into his cloak and set a large coin purse down on the desk by the door, then left without another word.

Her heart sank at his last words. *He will find me? Does this mean I really have no choice at all?*

# Chapter Five

It was an eternity later before she arrived home with her empty cart and mule. She was numb. What would her family say?

She took her time putting the cart away and making sure the mule was taken care of. She was in no hurry to face her parents yet. Once she was done, she double-checked the sheep were secured and fed for the night. She knew her father would've already done this, but one more time couldn't hurt.

When she left the barn, she was immediately greeted by an overly eager chicken. She smiled to herself; if anything could warm her heart right now, it would be her favorite pet. The animal had been her constant companion since she was young. As a chick, the hen was small for her age and had been picked on by the rest of the flock. Starlyn had understood how that felt and rescued the little thing. She raised her by hand and she followed her wherever she went. She sighed to herself. The chick was her only friend, really, and now she must leave her behind.

The animal excitedly clucked as it followed her to the house. Starlyn found herself standing outside, not wanting to go in yet. It was not the nicest of homes, but it was sturdy and full of love. She would miss it here. Mustering her courage, she finally decided she couldn't stall any longer.

The air seemed stiff, even tense, as she stepped through the threshold.

"Starlyn dear, is that you?"

Her heart nearly burst with sadness at the sound of her mother's voice.

"I'm home, Momma."

Her mother came from the kitchen, wiping her hands with a dish rag. Before Starlyn could speak, she wrapped her in a warm hug.

"Oh, my baby girl, we received great news today. Are you really being summoned to see the Elders?"

She nodded in return. If she spoke now, she feared she would only be able to cry.

"This is such an honor for you and the family. I know it's scary now, but you'll look back at this with pride one day." Her mother stroked her hair lovingly as she spoke. "Come get some dinner now, your father has been waiting."

They went to the table and Starlyn was shocked to see so much food set. There was a roasted chicken sitting next to a large meat pie. Included in the feast were boiled potatoes, carrots, and onions. She also spied some huckleberry cobbler. If her mother had prepared all of this, they considered this a celebration rather than a goodbye. She did her best to see it that way as well.

Her attempts fell flat as her father avoided eye contact with her. He took a drink from his glass. Judging by the face he made, its contents were something stronger than wine. Starlyn wished her glass was filled with something other than water.

The evening went on and much of it was spent in silence. She squirmed in her seat as her mother made obvious attempts to fill the silence. Her mother randomly spoke about being so proud and what items she should bring with her, listing silly things like a comb and dresses. Like she owned more than one dress or cloak. Her comb was poorly made from a piece of wood. Shame flushed her face at the thought of presenting herself in front of the Elders dressed in her rags.

"Don't forget to use your manners, child. You will be

meeting gods after all. Of course, you must not forget to smile, you are so pretty when you smile." She was rambling now, lost in her own musings. All the while, her father stayed completely quiet.

After the meal, she spent time with her mother, cleaning up and packing. Everything was surreal to her, like she was watching someone else performing the tasks. It was late into the night before she excused herself to lie down.

She lay staring at the ceiling for a long time as her chicken snored on her clothes chest on the other side of the room. Would she really stand before gods? Why would they choose her, of all people? She was nothing special. If anything, she would be considered less than average. There had to have been a mistake of some kind.

Panic began to bubble under the surface of her mind. Was it possible for her to refuse? Could she hide herself from them? An image of the Guardian flashed into her mind and she shivered. She could not hide from his eyes.

She lay there a long time before she heard the cloth at her door rustle, and her father walked in quietly. He sat on the trunk next to her pet chicken and sighed deeply. She thought he would speak to her, but he stayed silent, studying her in the dark while he thought her asleep.

"Papa?"

"Why are you awake, my girl?"

"I should ask you the same thing."

She sat up in bed and faced him. She was well aware why he wasn't asleep, just as he knew why she wasn't either.

"You don't have to go if you don't want to." He spoke quietly.

Her heart skipped a beat. Would it really be possible to

refuse if her father backed her on the choice? She wanted to stay here so badly.

The Guardian's threat back in her uncle's shop rang loudly in her mind now. He'd said he would find her if she ran. No, she could not refuse after all.

"I want to go, Papa. Just think of the adventures I'll have." She tried her best to sound genuine, but the words were hollow.

He rose from his seat and sat next to her, pulling her into his side with one arm.

"My brave girl, the world is not ready for your spirit," he teased. "You are so strong; I do not doubt you will bring great honor to us."

She smiled despite her fear. She would finally be able to explore the world she had only heard about in stories. Maybe this wasn't such a bad thing after all.

Her father kissed her forehead before leaving the room, and she flopped back down on her mattress. She clicked her tongue and called her pet hen to her. It responded instantly, nesting into her side and quickly falling back asleep.

Her heart ached as she pulled the animal closer to her. Could she really leave all this behind? Deep down, she knew she had no choice. The Guardian would take her with him no matter what. She needed to be brave and face this challenge head on. If not for herself, then for her family.

"I will make you proud, Papa ..." she whispered into the dark.

# Chapter Six

The dream started off like many of her dreams before. Starlyn found herself in her favorite field of flowers, playing with her friend hen. It was one of her happiest memories, and she replayed it often in her sleep.

It was a beautiful sunny day, and clouds drifted lazily across the blue sky. She sat cross legged, looking through the clover surrounding her. She was hoping to find one with four leaves, as it was rumored those were the lucky ones. Humming softly to herself as she searched, she happily worked her way through each single stem.

"The time has finally come."

She didn't stop searching for her clover when the faraway voice spoke; she was visited by the voices many times in her dreams and had learned trying to respond was pointless.

"Is she ready?" a second questioned. "Will she survive the change?"

"It is not for us to know. She is strong. I do not doubt she will learn to control her gifts soon enough."

"And what of her choice? Will she save them or damn them?"

Starlyn ignored the voices, ever searching for her clover.

"That is not for us to tell. The prophecy will be fulfilled, but the Dawn Child will decide in which way."

When the voices had gone silent again, she paused her search to watch her hen chase butterflies. She smiled inwardly, perfect contentment washing over her. After all, this was her favorite dream.

Something moved out of the corner of her eye. *Odd.* She didn't remember anyone else being in this dream. She glanced over and found a tall, slender woman standing in front of her. She jumped instinctively. Who could she possibly be?

She wore a light blue dress that flowed in a nonexistent wind and draped beautifully over her figure. Her bright blonde hair seemed to glitter in the sunlight, and her eyes were an icy shade of blue. She smiled warmly at Starlyn, holding out her hand.

Upon her palm rested a small clover with four leaves. She had found one! Starlyn was overcome with joy. Any doubts about the woman vanished instantly. She had found her a lucky clover. Starlyn gratefully accepted her gift, clutching it to her chest.

"Luck for your journey ahead." The woman's voice was almost melodic as she spoke. "I hope we shall meet again very soon."

"Good morning, sweetheart."

Starlyn awoke oddly refreshed. She fell asleep late into the night, but somehow was still renewed. Stretching her limbs, she yawned loudly.

"It's time for you to head back now, darling," her mother called.

The words didn't sink in immediately, but when they did, Starlyn's stomach seized as if she were about to retch. How had she forgotten? Today she was supposed to be leaving to meet the Guardian. The man who would take her to stand before the Elders. The thought made her shiver uncontrollably.

Her mother popped her head in, smiling brightly. "Don't take too long. We don't want to keep your Guardian waiting."

*My Guardian.* What a strange thing to say. Despite her fear, she smiled to herself. Maybe this wouldn't be such a bad thing after all.

She rose from bed as her mother clucked orders from the kitchen.

"Be sure to wear something warm, it's going to get cold tonight."

It all seemed too surreal. She dressed in a haze, her mind racing. Trying to be sure she forgot nothing important. Breakfast was a blur—did she eat at all? She couldn't remember, but she was sure her mother wouldn't have let her go without food.

Her father was absent this morning, already tending to the animals outside. Her heart ached at the thought of him working without her. She still had some time to help today, right?

She went outside and found him feeding the sheep. He spoke fondly to them as he went about his work. He always told her it soothed the animals when you talked to them, and it was something she did with every animal she encountered.

"Do you think they understand us?"

He didn't stop passing out feed when she spoke.

"I imagine they understand the feelings behind the words."

He was never much for deep conversations, but she loved being with him on the farm. She would miss this most of all.

She quickly grabbed an armful of hay and began doling it out alongside him. The sheep bleated happily, as if thanking her.

She continued helping her father in silence, just enjoying the normalcy of the routine one last time.

Once finished, they both drank deep from the water trough and surveyed their work.

"I have something for ya," her father said as he reached into his pocket. "It's not much but it's sturdy enough."

He handed her a small pocket knife. Not just any pocket knife, *his* pocket knife. The knife she had watched him use every day since she was young. She looked to him in disbelief.

"Now don't start that, girl. Every traveler should carry a knife. Since you'll be an adventurer now, I figured you better have one for yourself."

She smiled brightly at him before throwing herself into his arms for a hug.

"I will be the greatest adventurer ever. You'll hear stories about me soon enough."

Uncle Tomlin wasted no time as he busied himself with getting her ready. Her trip back to his shop seemed like a dream now. She barely remembered entering the city walls. Now she found herself at the mercy of her uncle, who insisted he help her pack as well.

Surprisingly, he was not red-faced with irritation. His eyes shone with something she did not recognize from him. Was it sympathy? He finally stopped packing long enough to wrap his chubby arms around her in a great big hug, shocking her with his closeness.

"Starlyn, I know you don't like this, but you must be strong for our family. It's up to you to show the Elders that our family is loyal." She could only smile in return. "Come now, child, I will not let you travel with nothing."

She followed blindly, still not understanding why she was the one to go. She sat down heavily as her uncle clucked orders to his workers. She held the letter the Guardian had given her the day before, afraid to read it. Maybe not reading it meant she could just pretend it wasn't real.

She turned the letter over in her hands, thinking about what her uncle had said, and broke the seal. The contents were disappointing.

It said much the same thing the Guardian did, which was only that an explanation would be given upon arrival and that all accommodations, transportation, and protection would be provided.

Deep panic bubbled to the surface of her mind. This was not going to happen. She couldn't just leave with a stranger, could she? Wiping the start of tears from her eyes, she put on a brave face. She took another deep breath and reminded herself to be strong for her family. This would change things forever. She was an adventurer now.

It wasn't long before she said her goodbyes to her uncle. She showed little emotion, but her hands trembled uncontrollably. She stepped over the threshold of the shop with a heavy pack slung over her shoulder and had no idea where she was going or why. This was all happening too fast. She reached for the little knife her father had given her and was comforted when she wrapped her hand around it inside her cloak pocket.

The day was muggy and grey, much like her mood. She glanced up and down the street, barely noticing the other people walking by, and at the same time they did not notice her. No one would miss her here. It was a bitter and lonely thought. As long as she could remember, she had wanted to travel the world beyond these walls, but she never imagined it would be alone, without her family.

A cold wind had begun to pick up as the sun got lower in the sky. Starlyn hugged her cape tighter while telling herself it was only from the cold.

When she glanced up again, she finally saw her new companion approaching. Seeing the Guardian made her hands begin to tremble once more. She swallowed hard. He was daunting as he rode up on a massive horse.

Starlyn had never seen such a beautiful animal in her life. The large stallion trotted with a lively step and tossed its head noisily at the passersby. She was awestruck by the black glossy coat shining in the fading light, proving that nature truly was an artist.

Trotting placidly alongside was a much more amiable brown mare, which she assumed was for her. The mare was older and very calm, her white mane drooping lazily into her face.

As the Guardian got closer, animals in the street nervously sidestepped around him. One horse nearly toppled the cart it was pulling in order to get away from him. People around her stared openly at the man in the white mask, and she started to understand the gravity of what was happening.

Her trembling spread to her knees, her eyes never leaving the man approaching her. When the Guardian gracefully dismounted and offered his hand, she stumbled back, feeling weak. His hand shot out, grabbing onto hers before she fell.

He assisted Starlyn as she mounted the mare. She kept her eyes low, trying hard not to meet his hypnotic gaze. Without any words spoken between them, they trotted south through the vast streets of *Groot Paleis*.

The South Gate was much less active than the North Gate, especially with night fast approaching. This made their departure out of the city quick and smooth. Sighing deeply, she glanced back at the walls of her past, not knowing if she would ever be with her family again. A gust of wind blew her thin cape into her face just in time to cover her tears.

# Chapter Seven

It didn't take long for the Necromancer's informant to bring him the information he needed. With his spies throughout the city, he barely had to lift a finger in order to find whatever or whoever he was looking for. Sometimes this was a blessing, and sometimes he found it incredibly boring.

The Guardian he hunted had left by the South Gate not a half hour ago. Just as expected, he was returning to *Hemel Deur*.

The most interesting part was that he had a local girl in tow, and if his informant was correct, which he always was, the Guardian was dressed in solid black. This meant that he was not just any ordinary Guardian—he was Elite.

Too many questions without answers surrounded this mystery. Who was the girl? Why was Pelf killed, and most of all, how had he completely banished the soul of the corrupt banker from this world and the Underworld?

The first question had led him into the upper regions of *Groot Paleis*, not far past the inner wall. He studied the ordinary looking tailor shop for some time, and after not finding anything interesting outside, Trust crossed the street to go inside. He was promptly greeted by an idiotically dressed, heavyset man.

"Good sir, I welcome you to Tomlin's Tailoring and Exports. How may I assist you?" He was unmistakably looking Trust over, measuring the depth of his purse.

Mimicking the little man's demeanor, Trust casually walked to the nearest rack of colorful fabric. The man followed closely.

"Is there something in particular you're looking for?"

Trust glanced at the man with indifferent eyes, pretending he wasn't interested in the conversation. "I have heard a rumor or two about this place of business and I had to see what all the talk was about."

The man obviously liked the idea of people talking about his shop. He puffed out his chest and bowed his head respectfully.

"I, good sir, am Tomlin DeTousan. I am the owner of this establishment, and may I be so bold as to assume you have heard how fine my craft is?"

Smiling triumphantly, the Necromancer bowed his head in return. "Is it true that you have had the patronage of a Guardian of the Elite?"

He was assured of his success when Tomlin began to glance around, clearly making sure no one else was listening. Tomlin leaned in closer and Trust copied his stance.

"I have made many garments for the Elders, but the most recent visit was special, oh yes, much more than just the need of my artistic ability with the needle. My very own niece was summoned to *Hemel Deur*."

The Necromancer didn't have to fake his surprise. Why would the niece of such a commoner need the protection of the Elite? This was beginning to become a puzzle worth solving.

"What a great honor, my fine man. Do tell me, why was she summoned?" Trust was starting to become impatient with this pompous man. He was wasting time.

"My good sir, I do not think this is a conversation I'm supposed to be having, but you look like a fine fellow who can keep a secret. I personally believe she will be rewarded for our loyalty. She is the only one available to respond without interrupting all my work, you know," Tomlin replied curtly.

Time was up and Trust didn't have the patience to listen to this man anymore. It was obvious he knew nothing of why his niece was summoned.

"Thank you, Tomlin DeTousan, for your hospitality. I will be happy to assure anyone who asks about your integrity and class."

Not waiting for a reply, the Necromancer left the shop, his mind already making a list of things he needed to do.

First, he had to get to a safe house so his work was uninterrupted. A few raindrops began to fall as he hopped over a nearby puddle. It was time to pay a visit to a few of his less than favorite demons. He had many favors that were long unsettled, but this would be one of the most important. If he worked fast, he would be able to delay the Guardian and the girl long enough to get to Cat's Cradle before them.

This day would be busier than he'd thought. He shrugged to himself, thinking he was long overdue for some traveling, anyway.

There were several locations around the city where Trust could take refuge long enough to delve into the Underworld. He had made sure each one was kept in the best condition and that no one else knew they were tied to him by using third party renters with false names.

Each safe house had pre-drawn protection ruins, ensuring he had everything he needed to travel smoothly and quickly to the Underworld. This had been beneficial many times, yet today it seemed exceptionally important for him to act quickly.

He set up fast, wasting no time laying out the right stones

and sitting inside the circle of ruins. The Guardian had a head start, and he'd need to delay him as long as possible so he would be able to get to Cat's Cradle first. In order to do that, he would recruit the help of a distraction, one that would delay their trip, yet not kill either of them.

He contemplated his choices before deciding on the perfect participant. A vampire would do nicely. They were easily distracted by humans, but not too difficult to kill. All that was left was to summon one. He sat cross-legged in his rune circle, focusing on the tenth gate.

He tended to avoid this gate; it was basically a false heaven, lulling you into believing you were in a happily ever after story. The demons here were alluring and deadly. They fed off of your secrets, desires, and sinful emotions. The perfect feeding grounds for vampires.

It had been a long time since he'd ventured to the tenth gate. Actually, he was a young boy the last time he was here. He found his thoughts beginning to wander and he tried to refocus. Shaking his head, he took another deep breath and imagined the gate once again.

This was the gate where he'd discovered his love for necromancy—if you could call an obsession with death love. His earliest experience with a vampire was when his family was attacked by one. He focused harder as he remembered the day it happened.

He was the youngest of three sons in a wealthy family. They had a carefree life, and he'd learned early on of his abilities to go into the Underworld, yet he had no idea how dangerous his visits had been. That is, until he was followed home one night.

It had been storming, which was rare in the southlands, and he had been afraid of the dark. He could still envision the flash of lightning; the thunder crashing left his heart racing. When he left his bedroom, he ran to his mother. She always knew how to soothe him during one of these scarce storms.

When he crept into his mother's room, he found she was not alone. He would never forget the horrifying sight of the vampire on top of his mother, claws grasping deep into her shoulder as its fangs pierced under her collarbone, gouging a hole where her heart should have been.

The creature smiled at him then, letting his mother fall to the ground in a heap before fleeing back to the Underworld. Full of rage, he followed the creature past the tenth gate with the intention of killing him.

Yet when he arrived, he found something much more valuable: his mother. She was his false heaven, a gift from the tenth gate. He swore he would find a way to bring her back with him. That was when he'd begun to learn necromancy. That was what started it all. His heart burned from the hurt of watching his mother die, only to find her again at the tenth gate.

He shivered. It was not good to live in the past, but every time he encountered a vampire he thought of that day.

Now he found himself in the presence of these nightmares again. He had made it to the second gate and immediately found himself standing in front of his mother's smiling face. She would always be his false heaven.

"You have come back for me," her voice sang out, so beautiful.

He walked past her without making eye contact. He had learned long ago this was not his mother, only a demon disguised as his mother. He didn't have time to waste with the creature. He had spent too much time with her memory already.

He pulled out his knife and sliced it across the palm of his hand. The easiest way to find a vampire was with blood. He let it run down his arm and puddle on the ground beside him as he waited. He was losing his patience, but finally his senses picked up on the smell of rot.

He sneered at the smell and met the eyes of the vampire standing before him. He raised his bloody palm to the creature.

"I have come to take you to the mortal world."

The monster hesitated. "Why?"

"There is a girl you must kill for me."

The foul creature pondered the choices he had, looking for the trick he was sure Trust was laying before him.

"I stay in mortal world if I kill girl?"

Trust nodded in agreement. The creature smiled a sickly grin, showing off its impressive set of razor-sharp teeth.

"Take me to the girl."

# Chapter Eight

As if the sky reflected Starlyn's mood, the rain had begun to fall as the city faded in the distance. She adjusted herself uncomfortably in the saddle. She was not used to riding a horse and her back was already starting to ache.

The sun was setting fast, and the rain was picking up speed. The wind cut right through her tattered cape, making tears start to well in her eyes again. She glanced nervously at the Guardian as he rode. The wind whipped his cape back behind him, yet he continued on with a straight back. If the weather was bothering him at all, he was very good at hiding it.

Starlyn shivered uncontrollably, hugging herself tight. A tiny seed of loathing began to grow in the pit of her stomach. She did not like this trip one bit, and she glared at the man who had forced her to be on a horse in the rain.

"What's your name?" she asked, breaking the long silence. She waited for a response and grew angrier when none came. "I asked what I should call you!"

"Guardian." He did not turn when he spoke.

Her anger and frustration bubbled over, but when she opened her mouth to speak, she was cut off by a horrific wail in the distance. The piercing screech came from the brush off the side of the road

As she turned to the noise, a black blur swooped down straight toward her. Starlyn screamed and her mount reared. Being inexperienced on a horse, she tumbled from the saddle and landed hard on her right shoulder.

The horse bolted immediately for the brush in the distance. She wheezed, desperate for air, but only succeeded in filling her mouth with mud. Coughing harshly, panic seized her. She could not breathe! Lifting her head, she hoped to find anyone to help her. Instead, she found the monster not even five feet away from her. Its red eyes glowed in the twilight and its sickly sharp teeth shone brilliantly when it smiled at her.

The smell of decay was overpowering. Starlyn tried to scoot away, gasping loudly as streaks of pain shot from her shoulder. She held back tears as the creature squatted, looking like some kind of horrible feline preparing to pounce.

There was nowhere to run, nowhere to hide from the dark beast. Her lungs burned for air and her heart beat so fast she was afraid it would explode. When the monster leapt into the air, she closed her eyes tight, hot tears running down her cheeks. Her heart was louder than the creature's howls as she waited for the killing blow. One, two, three ... Nothing happened.

Mustering her courage, she opened her eyes. The outline of the creature's body in the failing light was shocking. It lay on the ground so close, its arm outstretched toward her. She jerked her boot away from its clawed hand.

The Guardian stood over the monster with its severed head still in his grip. He dropped the head of the beast next to the slumped body and turned to her. When his eyes met hers, she held her breath. His mask stood out vividly against its black background of the night sky and she found herself retreating from his grasp. He was just as terrifying as the creature he had killed.

He knelt down beside her, patiently waiting for her to come back from the shock. A gust of wind blew back his hood, revealing a long golden braid trailing in the wind. The rain immediately soaked him and his loose strands of hair fell into his face, sticking to his mask. He gently held her shoulder, and

Starlyn winced when he prodded the most tender spots. With a quick and unexpected tug, he pulled her arm back into the socket, knocking the breath from her again.

Gasping loudly, Starlyn collapsed into his arms. The pain was blinding. He easily swept her up onto his horse. Without another glance back, he urged the graceful animal forward. Starlyn sobbed softly, her head nestled in his cape and his arms wrapped around her. Suddenly aware of their closeness, she jerked herself free from his hold, nearly falling from the horse.

"What the hells was that?" she screamed.

"A vampire."

Starlyn's jaw dropped. "They're not real, are they? I mean, not like in the stories."

He snorted at her question, which was the closest thing to a laugh she had heard from him. "You tell me. Did you not see it?"

She shuddered again, glancing around nervously and beginning to like the idea of her back being protected against him.

"Are there any more out here? Should we be getting inside or something?"

The horse took a few more steps before he spoke again.

"There will be no more tonight. We will stop soon at Cat's Cradle, though it will take us longer now with one horse."

She winced. He made it sound like it was her fault the horse had bolted.

"Once there, I suspect you will be able to wash off all that mud."

Her shame grew as she wiped her face in vain. It only smeared the grime worse. She was glad the night hid most of the mess.

It was a very uncomfortable eternity before the lantern in front of the little inn known as Cat's Cradle became visible. The Guardian had been right about the journey taking longer with one horse.

Riding a horse was terribly tiring, but riding double was even worse. Without stirrups to rest her feet in, her thighs burned and her calves had begun to cramp. Her back was stiff and her injured shoulder throbbed in time with the ache in her head. The sight of the inn was indeed a beautiful one.

The rain was finally beginning to subside as the Guardian helped her to the ground. Her legs responded poorly as she put her weight on them. This whole experience was amazingly embarrassing. First her rain-soaked and mud-splashed appearance, then her wobbly knees and her awkward limp. It was too much to wish that the inn would be empty when she walked in, but she hoped for it anyways.

Taking a deep breath, she prepared for the stares as she entered the inn. Instead of surprised looks, she was greeted by a pleasant wave of warmth and the most alluring aroma wafting from the kitchen. Her stomach's response was more powerful than all of her aches, pains, and fears. She was starving and wanted whatever they had to give her.

A stranger passed by her, then looked at her twice before interrupting her train of thought.

"My word, girl, are you okay?"

# Chapter Nine

The girl went inside Cat's Cradle alone and obviously stiff while the Guardian tethered his horse and unhooked his saddlebags. He would have to remedy her leaving him without permission.

A new horse would be needed for her before they could keep traveling. She was an amateur at riding, that was obvious. It would make for a longer trip than anticipated. The girl had already shown a temper, and she had an irritating way of hating you in silence.

The Guardian followed Starlyn into the inn and took in the entire scene immediately. There were three other patrons besides Starlyn and himself. Two were conversing with each other at a table in the back. They were harmless. The third was engrossed in a conversation with Starlyn. He frowned behind his mask. That was not something the Guardian wanted to allow to happen too frequently. The owner of the inn came forward and tilted her head in a familiar greeting.

"How you doin', honey?" she said warmly. "Looks like your charge is in dire need of a bath and a good bed."

The Guardian didn't bother to respond as he strategically sized up the newcomer. He was tall and slender with a fluid way of moving. He definitely had some training with weapons, or was possibly a soldier, judging by the way he stood.

His belt was mostly covered by his long, sleeveless jacket, but it was clear to the Guardian that he had no visible weapons on him. His dark skin and dark eyes meant he was southern born, and the small stones piercing his outer ears were also a southern tradition. Finally, he returned his attention to the woman next to him.

"I would like one room with one bed, my usual if it is available. The girl needs a bath drawn and some food brought up to the room. By any chance, have you seen any twins here tonight?"

Before the innkeeper could respond, she was interrupted by a sudden burst of laughter. His attention returned to the girl as she hugged the stranger with a wide smile on her face. The man awkwardly hugged her back with one arm, his eyebrows raised in bewilderment. Then Starlyn turned to the Guardian and almost skipped over to where he stood.

"This kind man found my mare! He says she was wandering nearby. Isn't that fantastic?" Starlyn said, flashing a brilliant smile.

The man walked over to the group, giving away nothing and hiding everything behind his casual smile. Starlyn beamed as she thanked the man again. She turned to the Guardian.

"Well, aren't you going to say anything? We should reward him or something," she demanded.

The Guardian met the stranger's eyes. The man was hiding something. It was a secret that he had hidden for a long time and the lie was now natural to him. The Guardian was trained to recognize people's secrets, things no one wanted him to see. The man's smile never faltered once under his scrutiny.

"Convenient," was all he said to the stranger.

Starlyn's smile had disappeared as soon as he'd spoken. Her hands were on her hips and her lips were tight as she glared directly at him.

"Allow me to introduce myself properly. I am Trust from the House of Riyaadh," the man said with a smooth bow that was just low enough to be polite but not subordinate. "I do not wish any reward, but perhaps the two of you would do me the honor of dining with me this evening?"

His eyes never left the sword that rested on the Guardian's back. Starlyn's smile returned and she was nodding in agreement.

"That will not be necessary. We have prior arrangements," the Guardian said in an even tone.

She opened her mouth to speak but was strategically cut off by the innkeeper.

"Come, love, I have a nice big bath all ready for ya. My name is Cat, my dear, and I'll make sure you are well taken care of. My niece will fetch your things and I'm sure some fresh clothes can be found."

Starlyn was trying to pull her arm out of Cat's grasp, but Cat was too smart to let go.

The glance he gave Trust was full of warning as he brushed by the man. Trust was after something, and he didn't like the man getting so close to Starlyn. Tailing Cat and her captive, he walked up the stairs to the very last room on the left side of the hallway.

When he surveyed the room they entered, he was pleased to find that it hadn't changed since the last time he was here. That was just the way he preferred it. A large bed was the focus of the room, it was not fancy but efficient. A chest sat at the foot of the bed and a small vanity with a mirror next to it. On the other side of the room was a table with one chair next to the cloth-covered doorway which led to the private bath.

Cat and Starlyn had already disappeared behind the curtain, and Cat's niece hurried past holding the once-lost saddlebags.

The Guardian placed his own bags in an empty corner of the room and began a more thorough survey of the items inside. He ignored the innkeeper's niece as she brushed by him, too close to not be deliberate.

He gritted his teeth, knowing that the sooner he got this over with, the sooner he could ignore her. *De Oudsten* were generous to their followers and the girl knew he would have gifts for her. As he trailed the girl, she overexaggerated the way she swayed her hips down the hall. She was young and foolish to think he would be distracted by flirting. The girl walked downstairs and into the kitchen, where she busied herself with the large roast hanging above the fire.

He waited for a few moments before he cleared his throat, and she turned as if she had forgotten he was there. Not wanting to waste any more time, he pulled out a sparkling necklace from his cape.

"As always, your loyalty is appreciated," he stated coldly.

She put her hand to her chest in mock surprise and lifted her hair from her neck. "If you would please do me the favor."

He ground his teeth together as he fastened it around her neck. She giggled as he did so, and when he had finished, she waved him away as if she had summoned him.

While in the kitchen, he made sure food was being prepared for the girl and finished giving out some gifts to the other employees. When he finally turned to go back to the room, he stopped at the sound of Starlyn's voice. He followed it into the common room and found her sitting with Trust, surrounded by food. The man began to play a flute and Starlyn became quiet. She stared at him in awe as he played.

The Guardian was hit by a wave of anger. The reaction was something he had not expected. Emotions were dangerous for him. She had left the room unaccompanied, and she was with a strange man. His blood began to heat up when she leaned in toward Trust slightly.

Was she really that gullible? Was she so juvenile that she would fall for the tricks of a smooth talker? Rage boiled inside him as he watched a smile glint in Trust's eyes. This would end now. With long steps, he crossed the room, not knowing exactly what his intentions were. He only knew that the man sitting there would not speak with Starlyn again.

# Chapter Ten

"I'm glad you decided to join me. I do hate dining by myself." Trust spoke gracefully as he poured her a glass of wine.

She took it gratefully and swallowed a large gulp before choking. The wine was not watered like she was used to, and so she smiled again to cover her inexperience.

"How could I refuse after you found all my stuff? I can't thank you enough," she replied after taking another, more successful, drink of wine.

She was out of place in the common room of the inn, especially alone without the Guardian. After she had been whisked away by Cat, she'd had a much-needed bath and a change of clothes. She came alone to find food but found Trust instead. He already had a massive spread of food at his table, and it would be incredibly rude to turn down his offer a second time.

"You look remarkably well this evening," he complimented her.

She flushed when she remembered the state she had been in upon first meeting the man. She glanced at her lap and was grateful for the fine new clothes she wore.

The rich green material of the vest was as soft as fresh butter and as sturdy as canvas, unlike anything she had seen before. She smiled as her hand went over the little silver buttons running down the front. The skirt was layered, with the same material as the vest used for the lining. The inside was sewn as a split riding skirt, which was much like a wide pair of men's pants, and a heavier earthy brown material was used for the final layer. The outer layer had matching silver buttons running up the front and back. This would give the illusion of a normal skirt when buttoned up or could be unbuttoned to ride in. All in all, it was a very modern outfit that cleverly went from practical to pretty with little effort, which Starlyn liked.

Her mind went to the letter she had found with the clothes and she smiled lightly to herself, remembering its contents:

*Starlyn,*

*I have had these items and others made for some time now. They were going to be a gift for the upcoming celebration of your adulthood. I am sorry that now I cannot give them to you there. I hope that they will prove useful as you fulfill this honor for the entire DeTousan family.*

*Sincerely,*

*Uncle Tomlin*

In one week, her coming of age celebration was scheduled. Thinking about how proud her mother had been when she spoke about the festivities made her heart ache. She would have to miss her own party. She had lived to see her eighteenth cycle of the seasons and would have the option to marry or become an apprentice. What would happen to her now that she was away? She would celebrate alone and too far away from either option. Starlyn sighed deeply as the wine began to muddle her thoughts.

Trust motioned to the food on the table and she helped herself to the sliced roast surrounded by boiled potatoes, onions, garlic, and thick gravy, then hungrily ate. After she was done with her roast and was moving on to a loaf of crusty bread, she moaned softly to herself, enjoying the warmth of the inn and the feeling of a full stomach. She glanced at the flute in Trust's lap.

"You play the flute, is it a hobby?" she said a little sluggishly.

Picking up the flute, he smiled fondly.

"It's my profession, my dear. I play for the pleasure of others and sometimes myself."

Starlyn tried to wash down a dry piece of bread, only to find that her cup was still empty. Trust kindly refilled it for the third time.

"Would you like to hear some music, dear girl?" he asked courteously, and Starlyn nodded happily, feeling very giddy from the wine.

He began to play. It started off with soft, low notes which were so comforting to her. She stopped in the middle of her next drink to listen. As he continued his slow tune, she became completely consumed by its melody.

She couldn't put her finger on it, but she recognized the song deep in her very soul. It was fluid like a river and smooth like polished stone. It reminded her of warm blankets on a cold night, or maybe the early morning sunrise. She wiped her mouth and smiled wistfully. Her eyes became heavy and all thoughts of the past or future were gone from her mind. She was completely at peace with the music.

The moment was interrupted by a *BOOM* on the table making her jump in her seat. It was a harsh way to be brought back to the reality around her. The gloved fist of the Guardian was still on the table where it had landed loudly. His eyes burned into Trust as he leaned close. Trust met his gaze easily and did not stop playing his instrument, only now the melody had moved to a lower and more ominous sound, almost mocking the Guardian.

"You will stay away from the girl. Do you understand?" the Guardian said, his hard eyes never leaving the man before him.

Trust finally stopped playing his flute and glanced above the Guardian's head to where the large sword sat on his back, then back to the Guardian, saying nothing in response. The Guardian stood up tall and grabbed Starlyn's arm harshly. Letting out a little cry of fear and pain, she was jerked up and forced to stand. Her legs wobbled drunkenly as he pushed her hard toward the stairs.

She turned as the Guardian reached for the sword on his back. When he drew the blade, a cold blast of air took her breath away. She exhaled sharply in a white cloud and blinked frost from her eyelashes. Her eyes widened and she blanched as the Guardian drove the sword into the table. It popped and cracked as it, and the contents on top of it, froze solid. Fear registered on Trust's face while staring at that brilliant blue blade. The Guardian leaned on the sword so his face was inches from the shocked man.

"Do you understand?" the Guardian repeated in a low voice.

Gaining some composure, Trust stood and brushed off the pieces of frosty food from his jacket.

"Of course," he responded.

Satisfied, the Guardian pulled the sword from the table and returned it to his back. Still in shock, Starlyn followed when he grabbed her arm and led her upstairs once again.

"That was reckless of you. You know nothing about that man or his intentions toward you," he said once they got to the room, his eyes as cold as the common room they had just left.

Starlyn opened her mouth and then closed it again. The wine was still thick in her head and her irritation was not fully gone from before.

"You left me here! You left me here while you flirted with that girl. You left me alone with no food. Was I supposed to stay here and starve?" she yelled bitterly, holding back tears just below the surface.

She would never tell him that Trust was the only kind face she had seen this trip, which was some comfort after the horrible day she had experienced. She would not let this stranger that stood in front of her know how terribly afraid she was.

"I mistakenly assumed you were not so naïve," he retorted, not reflecting any of the anger she showed him.

"Well, maybe you don't know a thing about me and you should stop pretending to." Her tone became higher pitched and embarrassment flooded her cheeks. He whipped to face her again, causing her to stumble back onto the bed.

"You must obey me, girl. It is my job to get you to the Elders safely, and I cannot do that without your help. Do you wish for your family to discover this dishonor?"

She sucked in her tears again. She was entirely too tired to fight him anymore.

"Fine, I won't disobey you again. Please don't tell the Elders of my disrespect today." She bowed her head, showing her deference to him.

"I will not," he said plainly. "*De Zoekers* will be here soon, and then we shall know more of what to expect from our travels."

*De Zoekers?* Starlyn tried hard to remember the translation of the words. She groggily went to ask the meaning, but discovered the Guardian had left the room. She would have to wait and see.

# Chapter Eleven

Trust stayed standing as they left the room. Glancing at Cat and giving her an apologetic look, he walked to his own room with as much dignity as he could muster. The Necromancer was not afraid of death—he had ways around that. What was reflected in the blade of that sword was beyond his comprehension; the souls of hundreds screaming for him to save them. They were tortured, bitter souls who would never know the gates of the Underworld.

He collapsed in the big, overstuffed chair and suppressed the shivers that followed on his heels. He had seen true death in that sword, a death he had not dreamed existed. Mortality for him was a very vague concept, yet now he trembled, feeling truly vulnerable for the first time.

He had not experienced something this strange in many years, and now his curiosity was piqued. He would not be called a respectable Necromancer if he didn't learn all there was to know about death and the ways around it. The sword the Guardian held was a new form of death, and he needed to learn from it.

Trust sat and stared at the ceiling for a long time, trying to figure out a way to keep up with the Guardian and, more importantly, the sword. His thoughts quickly turned to Starlyn DeTousan and her pretty smile and grey eyes. He smiled to himself, thinking of her walking in covered in mud and soaked to the bone. She was a very attractive young girl once she cleaned up a bit, and she might be his key to the sword.

He jumped up and went through his pack, tossing trinkets

out of the way until he reached the one he searched for. It didn't look like much, just a plain dull black stone, about the size of his thumbnail, hanging on a leather cord. He placed the necklace on the bed and retrieved his flute. He closed his eyes and played a long time while picturing her pretty smile. When he finally finished, the stone shone with a glossy glow. Its color had changed from dull black to a misty blue grey, just like her eyes. He smiled to himself before tucking the flute and the stone away, and sat back down to ponder the many questions that surrounded the girl and her Guardian.

His eyelids drooped and his head began to bob. When he opened his eyes, he knew he was not in the room anymore. He instantly recognized the dark forest which surrounded him.

He was at the third gate. It was a mysterious place to be, full of dark shadows and old magic. He reflexively went over the different ways around this gate, and then concentrated on the land around him. His gaze skimmed through the dense brush and tried not to focus on the subtle movement out of the corner of his eye. He knew the tricks this forest could play on you.

He was brought here for a reason. Few beings were powerful enough to pull another's soul into the Underworld from a sleep state, and fewer still would have picked this gate to meet.

He felt the shadows move before he saw them. The darkness advanced with impossible speed, forming into a shape Trust recognized. *Nacht Agenten*, the Mistress, had sent her favorite minion this time. He did not flinch when the Night Runner slid to a stop mere inches away. His head swiveled back to meet the eyes of the giant wolf that stood before him.

"How may I help you, Selene?" Trust asked gingerly. The wolf shifted its shape fluidly, forming into a tall, slender, and completely naked woman.

He remembered her curves well from previous meetings.

Her raven black hair fell past her knees and swayed teasingly around her calves. And how could he ever forget her brilliant blue eyes?

She smiled wickedly at him as he studied her body closely.

"The Mistress wishes to know where Pelf is. Why you are not in the city?" She spoke in a velvety smooth voice as she moved closer to him, nearly pressing her body to his. "What are you up to, little man?"

Trust took a deep breath and tried to ignore her advancement. Oh, how she loved to tease him.

"It is my own business why I left the city and no concern of yours. You may tell your Mistress I will bring her Pelf once I retrieve his soul as promised."

The Night Runner laughed coolly and walked away from him, swaying her hips seductively.

"Pelf is no longer important, but the girl the Guardian escorts is. Keep following them, and when the Mistress is done with her, she will give you the sword," she said over her shoulder with a smile.

She changed back into the hideous black wolf and trotted away again. Tiny tendrils of irritation spread through his mind. How had she known about the Guardian and the girl? More importantly, how had she known about his interest in the sword?

He normally would not subject himself to the petty orders of someone like this Mistress. He only associated with her because of the promises he made about certain people she'd already paid him to watch. This new development irked him, but at the same time produced even more questions in his head. His curiosity would be the end of him.

Trust sighed and pulled his flute off his belt. He didn't

have anything better to do at the moment, and his questions about the sword still nagged at him. Glancing around, he found the once vacant gate was slowly beginning to reveal some not so friendly demons flittering in the shadows of the deep woods. Rolling his eyes at some of the braver ones, he began to play the melody of returning. He would do what the Mistress wanted ... for now.

# Chapter Twelve

"Have faith, our child, have faith in *De Beschermer*," the voices whispered in her head. She knew them well, yet not at all. "There is hope for him. Have faith, our sweet child." Then the voices were no more.

Starlyn awoke to the dull thud of the door closing. Her eyes burned as she rubbed them. Had she slept at all? She sat up slowly, wincing not only at the pain in her shoulder but also the throbbing in her head. She moaned softly as she rubbed her eyes and began to become aware of the room.

She found a large platter sitting covered in the middle of the small table. Her stomach rumbled as she looked at the platter. She scooted off the bed and ran her fingers through her hair as she walked over to the table. When she lifted the lid, she was greeted by a variety of foods, which included boiled eggs, fried ham, warm fresh bread, and tea. Next to the tray was a small folded piece of cloth. Starlyn sat down and hungrily began to eat an egg as she unfolded the cloth. Inside, she found a beautiful stone on a leather cord and with it a note.

> *Starlyn DeTousan,*
>
> *It was a great pleasure to dine with you last night and I hope that I did not upset your Guardian too much. Please take this gift as an apology for my apparently bad behavior. I hope someday I can entertain you again. Until then, I hope your journey is swift and safe.*
>
> *Trust from the House of Riyaadh*

Starlyn smiled as she gazed into the cloudy stone. Worried

the Guardian wouldn't let her keep it, she tied it on her neck quickly. After the stone was securely in place, her headache was gone and she was suddenly rejuvenated. Shrugging, she went to her pack, chewing on her second boiled egg. Digging deep, she found what she was looking for. Instead of using the hot water for tea, she brewed her uncle's famous coffea and sipped it gingerly. Out of the corner of her eye, she caught a glimpse of the cloth to the other room moving.

Startled, she whipped around and found her Guardian staring at her while he pulled on his black gloves. This was her first time seeing him without his hooded cloak, so she took the opportunity to eye him up and down.

His hair was damp and freshly braided, falling neatly down his back. His black leather clothes fit too snug to his body, yet did not look constricting in any way. He wore five small knives on his upper arm, a curved blade about the size of her forearm tucked behind his belt, and a small hatchet strapped securely to one leg. Just like yesterday, all of this was accompanied by the sword at his hip and the sinister sword on his back. He looked every bit as lethal as she had witnessed him to be. When she finally peeled her eyes away from his body, she swore amusement flashed in those green eyes.

Her heart quickened and she quickly broke eye contact. She turned toward the mirror next to the bed, rubbing her shoulder and mumbling to herself. She sat down and wrapped her hair up into a bun. She was looking for something to secure her hair when she found the ink quill sitting in front of her. It was unused and from some kind of black bird. She shoved the quill into her bun and was satisfied that it would hold a few hours. Starlyn then grabbed her shoulder again, not thinking much about it.

The Guardian placed a small round bottle next to her on the desk. She nervously looked up at him with questioning eyes.

"This salve will help with the pain and quicken the healing," he said in a low and gentle voice that made her flush openly.

She sat a minute looking into the warped mirror, and after finally mustering the courage to swallow her pride, she turned to thank him but found that he had already left the room.

Looking at the table again, she picked up the little bottle and opened it cautiously. A familiar smell wafted from it, reminding her of sage and honey. She set the bottle down again, then quickly unfastened the buttons on her vest and took it off. When she slid down the sleeve of her chemise, she gasped at the large dark bruise she found forming there. It was much darker than she expected. She dipped her fingers into the bottle and rubbed the salve all over her shoulder, producing a tingling sensation wherever she applied it. Maybe she was truly being foolish last night. He had already saved her life once; it may be a good idea to listen to him better.

She was buttoning up her vest when the door slammed open, making her jump. Frowning, the Guardian briskly walked back into the room and was closely followed by two men. He was obviously angry, but not toward her. Who were these men?

# Chapter Thirteen

The Guardian walked down the hall to check if *De Zoekers* had arrived yet. It was hard to hide his irritation at their delay. He didn't want to stay here longer than needed, and it had been a long night of waiting.

He had been harsh on the girl. His duty was to protect her, but how was he supposed to do that without her assistance? She had fire in her soul, that he was sure of. He would have to deal with the girl differently to ensure her cooperation.

He shrugged, adjusting the sword at this back. The overwhelming hunger that coursed through the sword to him had become stronger in the last few days. Despite carrying the sword for years, it did not make it easier to wear.

The blade was his burden to bear, and if he did not control the sword, then someone else would use it wrongly. The hunger of the sword was untamable, yet he had found a way to coexist with it.

Entering the common room, he found Jack-obee and Jack-obide sitting casually together. They stood immediately as he approached and bowed in unison.

"Where have you been?" he asked, a bit annoyed by their nonchalant attitudes.

"We were delayed by the City Watch for the whole of last night, sir," Jack-obee answered flatly.

"Why?" the Guardian asked between gritted teeth.

"They believed we were spying on the current king for the

Elders."

His eyes narrowed at the news. How dare they imprison *De Zoekers* for something so outrageous? The new King would have to be given an example of how *De Oudsten* should be respected by all and feared like the gods they were.

"Come with me, I will hear your full report," he commanded as he turned back toward the room.

He entered without thinking about Starlyn, slamming the door open. He hated when pompous, feeble highborn had the audacity to disrespect their sacred faction of the Elders. He turned to the twins without looking at the girl once.

"Report," he commanded the twins.

Tearing their gazes from the girl, Jack-obee and Jack-obide both stood taller when he addressed them.

"We were on our way back from the girl's farmstead when the City Watch stopped us and questioned our motives. We did explain, as politely as possible, it was none of their concern. This made them a little upset. They decided that we were spies, giving them reason to arrest us."

"Well, after finding out about our arrest, a prudent general ordered our release, which happened early this morning before sunrise. We made haste to scout the next course of action," Jack-obee continued immediately after his brother had finished.

"The best path now is to follow the *Bloed Hout* until you reach the trading post *Vellei Bosje*. This should take you about a week. We will meet you there and advise on the next recommended route."

The Guardian nodded in agreement. He knew the trading post well and expected to be able to make it within a week's time or less. The girl laid on her stomach atop the bed, watching intently.

One of the twins cleared their throat, regaining the Guardian's attention.

"There is one more thing … There have been rumors reaching the city of farmsteads and ranches being attacked in the area of *Vellei Bosje*. All the families involved have disappeared, some say have been … eaten."

The Guardian huffed skeptically. Starlyn's mouth hung open, obviously shocked.

"You both know that rumors like that are common along the *Bloed Hout*. Why scare the girl more than she already is?"

The other brother shifted his feet uncomfortably before taking a deep breath and continuing. "The rumors also say *Nacht Agenten* are responsible."

The Guardian flinched hearing the name spoken out loud.

"*Nacht Agenten*? What does that mean?" Starlyn asked curiously.

"*Nacht Agenten* means Night Runners in the old tongue. Some would call them shapeshifters. Others know them as werewolves," the brothers answered in unison.

"Night Runners, here, that's impossible! They were run out of here decades ago," Starlyn exclaimed behind them.

The Guardian closed his eyes in annoyance as she jumped off the bed and approached the three.

"That's right, isn't it? They can't be in the *Bloed Hout*. They're extinct, just stories."

The Guardian sighed and opened his eyes to look at her. Knowing the truth was better kept restricted when it involved the *Nacht Agenten*, he would only tell as much as he had too.

"*De Oudsten* drove out or killed the packs of *Nacht Agenten* that lived in this land long ago. Most who survived headed north to the Bevroren Aarde. The specific use of these creatures in the rumors, when none have been seen in so long, makes it worth our time to listen. Rumors will always be rumors, but some start from truth."

She chewed her lower lip.

"You do not need to worry; I am here to protect you."

She met his eyes again and visibly relaxed. She glanced once toward the two *Zoekers* before nodding in agreement.

"I trust you," she said to him in a low voice.

Those three simple words gave him an overpowering urge to protect her, and he wanted to live up to that trust and more. He needed to get her to *Hemel Deur* as soon as possible, so he would make sure she was safe. He looked back to the twins.

"Then we will see you in *Vellei Bosje* at the Merchant's Inn."

# Chapter Fourteen

The two men left and Starlyn furrowed her eyebrows. She'd had a deep feeling the whole time they were in the room that she had met them before. She had learned very early to trust her instincts, but she couldn't place their faces. She turned back to the Guardian, who was studying her. Caught off guard, she smiled awkwardly. To her surprise, there was a smile in his eyes before he turned to the corner where his pack was located.

Seeing the platter of food on the table, she unceremoniously crammed another egg into her mouth. Then, grabbing another one, she arranged her own belongings. When she was finally finished and had straightened, the Guardian was waiting for her with his cape on and pack over his shoulder. She hoisted her own, then followed him into the hallway and down the stairs.

She glanced around the common room, holding her breath. Was Trust among the visitors this morning? She was mildly disappointed, but not at all surprised, to find that he was not. The Guardian said farewell to Cat by paying her with a heavy looking coin purse, then out the door they went. All three of their horses stood waiting for them. Starlyn approached the mare with a wary eye. She stroked its nose, then down its neck.

"Now, no more funny stuff, right? I wouldn't mind an easy ride today," she whispered into the horse's ear.

Walking around to the side of the mare, she placed her pack inside the saddlebags before mounting. The mare sidestepped a few times before Starlyn gained control. Turning the mare, she found that the Guardian was mounted as well, with his stallion completely under control. With the packhorse in tow, they started down the road heading toward the *Bloed Hout*.

Far in the distance, past the farmsteads and orchards, there was a wash of deep red. The leaves of the maple trees which made up the *Bloed Hout* were just beginning to turn orange in patches in response to the colder weather. Seeing this, she finally understood why it was called the blood wood and she could honestly say that she had never imagined it would be so immense. She mentally began to run down the list of the horrible stories and monsters that she had heard about in those woods and wondered what kind of adventures she would have today. Yesterday there was a vampire and a mysterious minstrel, today the identical brothers with one blue eye and one green. What was left for tomorrow?

As they traveled, Starlyn took in the countryside with a hungry interest. She hadn't traveled far beyond *Paleis Schaduw* and *Groot Paleis*, but she had listened to thousands of stories about the world from travelers. The world was one giant collection of tales in her mind, and she was ready to add her own adventures to those stories. She loved seeing the many apple and pear orchards up close. Normally, she guessed, they were not that exciting, but right now it was harvest time and that kept everyone busy.

The men and women worked together, some in trees while others stayed on the ground. The process was fascinating. Strong men climbed to the tops with big canvas bags and filled them full, then passed them down to their friends. They passed small family orchards where children played in the trees, then came to larger and wealthier estates where the children would be home with nannies. She smiled wistfully; everyone was busy working but her. She should be at home right now, feeding the sheep and making sure all were accounted for. At least the Guardian had promised to get her family help.

Her mind was wandering when her eyes fell upon one particular body high in a tree. The man was not much older than Starlyn and he was sitting comfortably in his perch, working hard like all the rest. His shirtless back was covered with sweat from a long morning's work. She stared at him for a long time before they reached where he was.

He turned to see the nature of the riders and smiled. Her face began to heat up as she returned his smile. She rode past, trying hard not to glance at the man, but when he caught her looking again, he winked and tossed her a large apple. She beamed brightly at him while waving in thanks. As she enjoyed her gift, she realized the man did not care about the Guardian riding beside her. That made her happy, knowing that the Guardian was not as menacing to others as he was to her. She was worried people would shy away from her more when she was with him.

Soon, the orchards grew farther apart and the sun higher in the sky, and Starlyn found herself utterly bored. No grand adventure yet, unless you considered hunting the flies that landed upon her mare's back. Her companion was still silent as a stone and the quiet was becoming tedious.

With a surge of courage, she urged her horse up next to his and did not hide her interest in him. She eyed him up and down for the second time today, taking in all that he was and thinking of the things she could not see. She was ashamed for the events leading to today and hoped she could regain some respect from the man who traveled with her.

"Why do you carry two swords? Wouldn't one be enough?"

He sighed to himself, as if she was a child he had to deal with.

"They both have different purposes."

She nodded, pretending to understand what he was

talking about. The subject was one left for another time and she moved on to the next question.

"Why do you wear the mask?"

He kept his eyes forward as he spoke, straightening his back while raising his head higher. "It represents many things. For some it is a standard, much like a flag, to show allegiance to *De Oudsten*. To others, the mask makes them a part of something bigger than themselves. Skeptics believe it is a form of control used to prevent Guardians from gaining independence. One thing is certain and that is the mask is used to intimidate those that do not follow the old ways. It is a symbol of safety for our allies and a promise of death for our enemies."

Starlyn understood those reasons and all were fairly obvious, but her gut said none of those were his reason for wearing the mask.

"Why do *you* wear the mask?" she asked again, easing her horse closer to his, nearly touching his leg with her own.

He was silent for a long time. Had he not heard her? Before she could ask again, he turned to her and they locked eyes.

"The mask represents duty, discipline, but above all else it represents honor."

Starlyn saw endless loyalty and truth behind the walls of his soul, and deeper was the brief flicker of sadness. As she stared at him, seeing a glimpse of the man he was, she yearned for that kind of passion. It made her existence feel lonely and empty in comparison.

She was the one who looked away first, and all questions she could have asked faded away as her thoughts traveled inward. How would she ever earn the respect of such a man?

# Chapter Fifteen

A cold wind had started up after they passed the last orchard, and with the wind came the clouds, small on the horizon at first, then growing and darkening as they got closer to them. Starlyn's stomach rumbled softly, reminding her that she craved a hot meal.

They had stopped briefly by the side of the road earlier for a lunch of cheese and bread, but that was ages ago. On top of her chills and hunger, she was terribly sore from riding. Her thighs stung from the saddle and her shoulder was beginning to bother her again. She steeled herself to ignore all of this and trotted on.

As if reading her mind, the Guardian suddenly stood in his stirrups, looking to the side of the road. She mimicked his posture as she tried to see what he did. He turned his mount toward a small aspen grove not far from them and didn't bother to wait for her to follow.

She wished for a farm or an inn but none were in sight. They would camp in the grove. Sighing, she followed reluctantly, and by the time she caught up, the Guardian was dismounting in a small clearing by a smaller brook.

It didn't take long for him to unload their gear and brush, feed, and water the animals. As he did all of that, she gathered any dry tinder she could find to build a fire. An annoying drizzle had begun, and she threw up her hood, pushing down her irritation. She glanced around, looking for a spot to sleep out of the rain. Meanwhile, the Guardian began twisting and pulling a square piece of material. Curious, she dropped her bundle of wood and walked to where he stood. The cloth he was playing with was a perfect square with metal eyelets along the edges.

"What's that for?" she asked.

He began to tie four ropes through the holes in each corner of the cloth. He glanced at her once, then tied one rope to a nearby tree.

"It is our shelter from the rain," he said, like it was the most obvious thing in the world.

She stared at him, thinking that he was crazy as he pulled on the opposite corner rope. Her mouth dropped open as the small cloth stretched the length of the clearing where he tied it off on another tree. He did this with the other two ropes, and the final outcome was a tarp that stretched across the whole clearing. More than a little amazed, Starlyn walked under it and ran her hand across the material, finding that it was hard, stiff and felt thick and durable.

"How'd you do that?" she asked, not bothering to hide her astonishment.

He snorted once and pulled a fallen tree that was taller than him into the center and propped up the middle of the tarp with it.

"It was a gift from *De Oudsten*. I do not know how it works or why, I just know that it does. Weather, fire, or blade cannot harm it easily, and I have found it more than useful since I have owned it."

Uncle Tomlin would never believe her when she told him of this. Then again, he may just try to buy the artifact for himself. The sudden pang of loneliness surprised her. She missed him.

She returned her attention to the Guardian, who easily started a fire close to the middle of the makeshift tent. Feeling a little useless, she scoured the area for a place to sleep. She used her shoe to brush away the leaf litter near the fire. The Guardian handed her a very fluffy and clean bedroll. She began to feel guilty about her irritation earlier, but as she sat down near the fire, her guilt fled as every ache in her body revealed itself.

"This is some kind of cruel torture, you know that, right?" she said as she rubbed her inner thighs tenderly. Then a sudden stab of pain from her shoulder made her reach for that instead.

The Guardian kept his gaze on her, and with a worried look, he unclasped his cape. Then he squatted next to his bags and pulled out the jar of salve she used earlier.

"It is not meant to be torture. Let me put this on your shoulder," he said as if he did not expect a protest.

Her lips pressed together as she crossed her arms. "I decline the offer. I do not think that would be necessary or appropriate."

He shook his head at her stubbornness.

"I need to check if it is fractured," he said, obviously not caring if she was uncomfortable or not.

Starlyn prepared herself for a fight, but found herself too exhausted to do so. Besides, he did have a point, she thought to herself as she nodded in agreement. She closed her eyes and undid the top buttons of her vest. She carefully slipped out her injured arm and slid the chemise off her shoulder. She envisioned the dark bruise on her shoulder. Why was she here again?

His leather pants creaked as he sat on his heels next to her and she opened her eyes. He pulled off his gloves and dipped his fingers into the jar and began to lightly rub the ointment into her shoulder. She winced slightly and he pulled back.

"I'm fine, really. Please … finish."

She closed her eyes again as he began to work in the oily substance.

She tried to focus on happier things when he began to move her arm back and forth. She tried and tried to ignore the pain, thinking of warm beds, hot foods, and her mother's smile. None of these distracted her enough. He was feeling the joint now and this was the worst of it. She focused on the crackle of the fire and the trickle of the rain. Finally, she focused on the smell of leather and mint. She opened her eyes and stared at the Guardian as he worked. Had he always smelled of mint? He glanced briefly at her, then stopped and met her gaze.

"You smell good," she whispered.

His eyes widened slightly, then he looked down. "I am finished. You seem fine. I suppose you would like some food now."

He put his gloves back on and then she straightened out her own clothes.

"What did you have in mind?"

She stood to follow him. He stopped abruptly and she ran right into him as she was buttoning her vest. She glanced up sharply, feeling the fluttering of anger in her stomach, but her anger turned to shock when he handed her the large curved knife from his belt. She took it from his hand. It was heavier than she expected. The grip was too large for her smaller hand.

"I will find you something fresh, but it means I must leave for a time. Do not worry, this is only a precaution. You will be safe here. I give you my word. You can return the blade when I get back."

Swallowing the brief tingles of fear, she smiled at him slyly. "What if I don't want to give it back?" she teased, and was pleased at the smile in his eyes when he turned to retrieve his cape.

He glanced back just after he reached where the light from the fire ended. She sucked in a breath as the fire lit up his eyes, much like a wild animal's would reflect light. She did not exhale until he was gone, but could not shake the memory of his glowing eyes surrounded by the darkness.

# Chapter Sixteen

He left her there in the firelight, gripping the oversized blade he had used to end many men's lives. It was odd in her innocent hands. He was told to not leave her alone, but she made him strangely uncomfortable tonight. He'd adjusted to her temper now, but the rest of her was still strange. He wanted to take care of her. She put on a strong face but she was, in truth, very inexperienced to the world around her. That made her more vulnerable than he had expected, and he found himself very indulgent of her innocence, not wanting to allow that piece of her world to be destroyed just yet.

He shook his head roughly, as if that act would help him clear his head. He refocused again on the task before him and that was feeding his charge. He had quickly picked up on the scent of a wild hare that was closer than he had hoped to find something. He stalked it silently, not disturbing any brush around him, concentrating on staying in the shadows of the night. It was pitch black without a moon, but he could see perfectly. There were benefits to being a monster. He caught a flash of fur out of the corner of his eye. His hand found one of the small throwing knives on his arm, and with a flick of his wrist it was gone. He smiled to himself when his ears were greeted by the successful thud of steel in flesh.

He stood from his crouch and retrieved the blade from the rabbit, wiping it clean on the soft brown fur. He kneeled and began to clean the animal, trying not to think of the girl he left behind, but with no success.

She was not like others he had escorted, who were

wealthy, powerful, or even occasionally royalty. Most of that type would complain constantly while they ordered him like a servant and she did neither. It was an adjustment that was harder to make than he would have expected. In the past, he'd quietly pushed his charges into place, using his own intimidating position to quell their complaints. Starlyn was the first person he escorted to ever honestly yell at him without fright behind her voice. Almost as if she did not recognize she was supposed to fear him. Maybe that was why he desired to please her, maybe her naive looks made him feel the need to protect her. After skinning the hare and ignoring that baffling train of thought, he headed back to the clearing where he should not have left Starlyn alone.

When he arrived, he found her pacing around the fire, nervously glancing into the darkness. She obviously didn't like the idea of being alone in the dark. He made sure he was making plenty of noise as he walked up so he would not startle the girl. The trick was not enough, judging by how quickly she turned to him, holding the blade shakily with both hands and white knuckles.

Once she recognized it was him that approached, she visibly relaxed, letting the blade drop to her side and flashing the wide grin he had seen her give others but never him. The Guardian casually walked past her and set his kill near the fire. He then turned to her and leaned in as he reached for the knife, ignoring the fact that she did not move away from him. She let go easily despite her earlier jest, and he returned his knife to his belt.

It didn't take long for him to make a skewer for the rabbit and he squatted near the fire, making sure his prize did not burn. Starlyn sat opposite of him on her bedroll and let her hair out of the bun. She ran her fingers lazily through it and it was obvious the road was wearing her down quicker than he had hoped. Her eyes were ringed with dark circles and her lips were cracked from the wind. He had to remind himself that she was a sheepherder before this and always had a good meal and a warm bed to return to every night.

Before long the rabbit was ready to eat and the Guardian found himself cutting the meat off the bone for the girl. She had not asked him to, but he did it anyway. His efforts were rewarded by a very grateful smile as she shoved a strip into her mouth. She giggled to herself as grease ran down her chin. Wiping it away, she looked at him and swallowed.

"You're not eating? It's really good."

He never understood why his charges always asked that question.

He sighed. The truth was always the best route. "I do not require food or water. *De Oudsten* has provided me with a volunteer that willingly channels his consumption to me."

She chewed slowly, appearing to consider his words. Realization flickered across her face as she suddenly coughed, briefly choking on her rabbit.

"Wait—what? You're saying that a man volunteered to give you the nutrition from the food that he eats and drinks. What happens to the man if he gives all of his food to you?"

It was better to leave out the parts about the volunteers that died from starvation and dehydration.

"There is usually more than one, and the mages of *De Oudsten* who cast the link can easily monitor them. They are in charge of the health of the volunteers." Few mages in service to *De Oudsten* cared if the men lived or died as long as the Guardian stayed healthy for the duration of their mission.

But as a servant sworn to *De Oudsten*, it was not his concern about how it was accomplished. He was here to follow orders. The sacrifices of those people made the missions even more important to him, and he was proud that he always finished his missions quickly. Starlyn's mouth hung agape, and he was sure that she had many more questions. Finally, she closed her mouth. Her argument would be wasted upon him. She finished her meal in the quiet they were both becoming accustomed to.

He stood again and walked to where the horses were tethered, double-checking the work he knew was flawless. His horse nuzzled him familiarly while he tried to figure out why he was avoiding the girl's company. When he turned back to the camp, Starlyn was in mid-yawn, lying on her side toward the fire. The shadows flickered across her face, and she was suddenly something more than just a young peasant girl. She had a simple beauty he'd never noticed before because he never really took the time to truly look at her. How strange he hadn't seen it before. She propped her head up with her hand and returned his stare for a moment.

"Let me guess," she said sarcastically, "you have volunteers that sleep for you too."

He solemnly nodded and she rolled her eyes, then she rolled over, exposing her back to him.

He waited there a few moments, then left the horses and walked a few paces into the grove of aspens. When he was sure he was out of sight, he pulled out a piece of polished blue calcite and rolled it in his palm while he debated if the girl was asleep yet. Deciding he was safe, he began to rub the stone between his hands and before long it began to glow slightly. He casually tossed the stone onto the ground and waited. Soon the light of the rock grew brighter, eventually lighting the whole area around him. The shadow of a man began to form in the light, and then take more solid shape. He recognized the mage in the light and was not looking forward to the conversation he was about to have.

"You are late," the man said angrily once he recognized the Guardian. "*De Zoekers* made contact two days ago with news of the girl. Why have you failed to report?"

The Guardian regarded the slight man with distaste. He had always loathed this man and hated the authority the mage often abused. He was chosen by the gods, *De Oudsten* themselves, but he lacked the integrity to have his respect.

"As you have said, Iridium, *De Zoekers* have reported already. I am sure they promptly informed you of all the same information that I have. I am not contacting you to report. All I need is information on the rumors of *Nacht Agenten* in the area."

Iridium began to tremble as he held back his anger.

"You have been ordered to report daily. As *De Beschermer van de Elite*, I would expect you to know your place in our hierarchy. You will report daily, and I will make sure I personally receive your reports!"

It was hard to hide that he enjoyed it when the man lost control.

"Now, tell me about the girl. Does she talk about strange dreams to you? Has she mentioned anything out of the ordinary? You give me information and I will give you some in return," he said testily, balling his fists at his sides.

This would be pointless unless he cooperated, so he would comply for now.

"The girl talks in her sleep. She speaks about many things while resting, mainly about her home and family. The usual odd things, you know ... dream things. She asks a lot of questions when she is awake."

The mage listened intently to what the Guardian had assumed was useless information. The mage nodded, satisfied.

"The *Nacht Agenten* rumors have been confirmed.

Witnesses have said that a pack of seven, maybe eight, have been stalking the area around the *Bloed Hout*. You must be careful when dealing with these ones. They are not a creature you have dealt with before."

The Guardian snorted at him. The mage knew very well that his experience with *Nacht Agenten* was much more personal than most. He cocked his head abruptly, popping his neck. Starlyn began mumbling in her sleep and it was time to end this conversation.

He stepped forward and reached for the stone, and the mage's face contorted with anger as he picked it up. The stone immediately stopped glowing, and he enjoyed a moment to ponder what the mage would do about his leaving the conversation without being dismissed. The night was eerily black again, and it took a moment for the Guardian's eyes to readjust before he walked back to camp.

He ignored the rain as he took a position outside of the firelight. He squatted on his heels with his back against a tree as Starlyn tossed in her sleep. He listened to mumbling, but could not understand a word of it. Leaning his chin on his chest, he listened to the music of the night, paying close attention to anything that was not supposed to be there. He would sit here until dawn if everything went as planned. His only concern now was the sudden appearance of *Nacht Agenten*. He did not believe it was a coincidence that they resurfaced around the same time the girl was coming to age.

Despite his misgivings, the girl would be safe with him. There was no one better equipped to handle the *Nacht Agenten* than the creature that traveled with her now.

# Chapter Seventeen

Starlyn dreamed horrible dreams. Endless dreams where she was running through a barren landscape dotted with shrunken, malformed trees which cast a black silhouette on an already black environment.

She ran from a fear which choked her like smoke. Her legs were on fire from exhaustion. Soon the shadows around her were moving with her; the faster she ran only made them hungrier. Their cold hunger went deep into her bones and every step made her want to scream with dread. Without a doubt, she was running from wolves, wolves that were hiding in shadows. There was a howl in the distance, and she stumbled to the ground. They weren't just ordinary wolves, but monstrous ones with an appetite for death and pain. She could feel their eyes on her as they savored the smell of her fear.

She cried out to the voices that were always there, but they did not answer. She begged out loud for them to talk to her, to explain what was happening and why she was alone. No answers came.

The dark hillside was barely lit by the full moon. Huge shadows moved closer to her, their eyes reflected in the moonlight. Her terror became so overwhelming she wept. She wept for sanctuary and she wept for her lost soul, but most of all, she wept because she was alone. That was a feeling she would never be used to, the emptiness of being utterly alone. The voices were always there to help her escape the dreams, but tonight they abandoned her to the wolves.

She closed her eyes and felt out with the instincts that

she knew would never leave her, and she sensed the disfigured animals everywhere as they got closer. She reached out further.

There was something else, something vaguely familiar. She called to it; she called with all her heart and hoped it would help save her from these monsters.

# Chapter Eighteen

Trust always took pride in his ability to use the gifts he was given, especially when pertaining to the Underworld, yet he sometimes found his skill level made things boring. There was a time when it had taken a lot of energy for him to bind a lesser demon to his will, but now he had the practice and tools to easily conquer the task.

In this case, he was able to coax a demon to spy for him. It was a rather simple-minded demon he had chosen, one that would obey easily and hide even easier. This little devil was perfect simply because it was the size of a child's doll and moved at rapid speeds from shadow to shadow. The most important thing was that it would follow its mark until it or its mark died.

To top it all off, Trust had access to call the creature back to this realm for a report whenever he saw the need. Overall, he was pleased with his work when he unleashed it unto the world and was confident that the one task on its small demon mind would be carried out. Starlyn DeTousan was not the most threatening target to follow, but she was important nonetheless. Why? He could not figure it out yet, but perhaps with the help of his newest spy, he would determine why she was so important. Even more so, how to profit from it.

He was done in the realm of the dead, so he pulled out his flute, bringing it to his lips. Suddenly, there was fluttering in his stomach and a sudden need to go toward the left. *Odd.* There was nothing that way. He tried again to play his flute, but the urge to travel farther into the gate became stronger. He could not say why, only that it was the right direction to go and that he should hurry. Inquisitive as always, he complied, trotting lightly toward the source of the buzz. The closer he got, the more urgent the feelings were, and soon he was running full speed toward a giant unknown.

The absurdity of the situation did not go unnoticed. He was being foolish by continuing. Despite all his instincts screaming at him to stop, he kept going.

It didn't take long for him to find himself standing in front of what was known in the Underworld as a dream hole. They formed a sort of tunnel into someone's dreams, and often these holes were dangerous for the dreamer. Having a link directly to death allowed the dreamer's soul to wander, and getting lost in the Underworld was not a good idea. Furthermore, demons had a tendency to enter a hole in order to feed from the person or even to possess them.

He was reluctant to enter the endless black within the hole. It was never a good idea to venture into someone's dreams. He personally did not like the fact that too many things were out of your control when in someone else's dream. The feeling pushed at him to enter. His curiosity won over in the end, and he stepped cautiously into the unknown. He walked for a long time in complete darkness and began to worry about finding his way back. Instinctively, he reached for his flute, double-checking it was still there and all the while knowing this was a mistake.

Finally, after what seemed like hours, the shadows of objects in the dark started to take form, but he could not make out what they were. Soon a full moon became visible, resting high in the sky. Strangely, it cast no light on the surrounding environment. It didn't take him long to feel the presence of the demons that had beaten him here, and he recognized that they were common dream hunters, the kind that fed on human emotion. These ones apparently preferred fear and pain rather than pleasure. How many were here? Their numbers were enough that they would kill the victim in order to get their fill, that was for sure. The demons were not yet aware of his presence and that was exactly how he liked it.

As he continued on deeper into the darkness, a white shape began to take form in the distance. As he got closer, he discovered the shape was a girl. She was lying on the ground sobbing, her long white dress pooled gracefully around her. Surrounding her were at least twenty demons in the form of wolves and they were closing in.

This was the call he had answered; this girl had called him to help her. The power she must possess was astounding. It was not a simple task to will someone to you, especially from the Underworld into a dream. His mind instantly filled with questions he had for her, but first he had to banish the beasts.

He quickly retrieved his flute from his case and debated for a moment the best song to entrap the monsters with. If he played the wrong song, they would either flee or attack and he did not like either option. He took particular pleasure in banishing feeder demons past the twelfth gate, where they could not return without permission from the ruler of the Underworld himself.

Above all else, he would have to ensure that it was directed only at the demons and make sure that it would not affect the girl, for that would lead to her death by his hands—something he was not prepared to deal with.

Finally, after tossing around some ideas, he settled on a song that would be effective. He took a deep breath and began to play a slow, soft harmony that reminded him of a lullaby his mother once sang. It was sad to think that such a peaceful memory would be used to hypnotize feeder demons.

He watched the girl out of the corner of his eye as she raised her head in astonishment, as if she did not expect him to be there. That meant she did not know what she had accomplished. He filed that away in his memory and focused again on the task at hand.

The demons reacted much the same way as the girl as they drifted slowly in his direction, entranced as he had hoped. When they were as close as he felt comfortable, he carefully reached into his pouch and retrieved a small piece of black quartz, which would create a path for the transition into death. By that time, the demons were beginning to awaken from their stupor and were not happy about the distraction he had caused.

He fumbled slightly, almost dropping the small stone. Before any demon could act, he threw the quartz in the middle of the mass. A blinding flash of red light followed. His eyes watered in response. He closed them tight as he whistled the tune that would send them past the final gate. When he finally opened his eyes and focused again, he was pleased to find that every demon had been successfully banished.

He smoothed down his jacket before turning to the girl. She obviously had some sort of gift to be able to call him here nearly against his will, but she did not recognize it. Raw potential was always fun to work with and, if he played his cards right, then her potential could be his.

As he walked toward her, the sun was beginning to rise on the horizon. Now that the demons were gone, the girl once again had control over her dream and evidently did not like the dark.

She stood then, facing him. Suddenly, she didn't look so helpless. Her dress and her long brown hair floated around her lightly in a nonexistent wind. Before he was ten feet from her, he stopped, realizing that he recognized this girl. It was hard to fathom how this meeting couldn't have been more opportune. He resumed walking, and by the time he finally reached her the sun was high in the sky, illuminating her eyes. He smiled warmly at the girl.

"I know you." She gasped, her mouth wide in disbelief. "I know you!"

He smiled a bit more brightly at her, enjoying the moment a little longer before he spoke. "Starlyn DeTousan, I would be lying if I said that I was not myself surprised to find you here."

He bowed to her politely, not sure how to start this conversation. He would not waste this moment. Luckily, she took the liberty of coming up with a question first.

"How's this possible ... How'd you get here?"

"That is what I was going to ask you, my dear. I believe that it was you that called me here. So then ... how did I get here?"

She was confused for a second, then reached up and ran her hand through her hair in frustration.

"I was lost in the dark. I was running away from those wolves. I don't understand it, I was just paralyzed by the fear. I gave up ... after I fell here. I knew that I was going to die. I just knew that the monsters would consume my soul. It just seemed that simple. I would lay here and they would kill me."

She turned from him, covering her mouth with her hand.

"I remember closing my eyes and seeing inside the wolves. It's so hard to explain ... I saw the blackness inside them and I was surrounded by it. It was darker than the night. It was endless.

"Then I saw a light far in the distance, just like a star in the sky. The light gave me hope. I knew then I couldn't give in. So, I pulled the light to me. I wanted to be warm next to it. I wanted to feel protected. I pulled with all my heart, and the light grew brighter. I don't think the creatures saw the star coming. They thought they had won, but when I looked at that light, I knew they hadn't."

She faced him with furrowed brows.

"That star ... that light ... was you."

His next move was crucial. He didn't need to give away all the details. Starlyn had done something extraordinary, yet she was completely unaware. He may be able to use this to his advantage. If he finally got close to the girl, he would get close to the sword.

He glanced around only to find a grey hooded form on the horizon. His gut clenched tightly at the sight of this new intruder. There was only one way to win a fight with this kind of demon and that was to run. Others were approaching at an impossible rate; he had been here far too long and they had finally caught up to him.

Starlyn also began to notice the newcomers, and her eyes grew steely with anger. It was obvious that she was better prepared to deal with trouble now that she was ready for it. If she only knew the nature of these demons she would not be so bold.

"Starlyn, please forgive me, but my time here is incredibly short. These creatures are here to kill me and neither you nor I can do anything about it. This world you are in is merely a dream to you, but to me it is something else. Next time you need help, just remember that you control your dreams. I will return here soon. I promise you that."

"Please don't leave yet. I will make them go away."

He shook his head at her and grasped his flute. The figures were very close now—it was time for him to go.

He spoke again, this time to the ones that hunted him. "You were so close my friends, but alas I will not be so easy."

With that said, he began to play the song of returning and slipped out of their grasps again.

His last sight was of Starlyn squaring her shoulders to the faceless men, her jaw clenched with determination. He hoped she would not try to confront them on her own. Would she really be that foolish?

# Chapter Nineteen

Starlyn was not helpless anymore, but when she saw into the black abyss inside the hoods of these newcomers, fear crawled down her spine.

"What do you want with him?"

She threw her hands up while raising her voice. They ignored her and began to vanish one by one, making her blood boil.

"Tell me why you are here!"

Grabbing the nearest one just as it disappeared, she was suddenly no longer in her dreams. She had made a horrible mistake. All around her there were people in chains. Far on the horizon were men, women, and even children being tortured by the same grey hooded men. They all stopped at once and faced her. She sucked in her breath, and then coughed it out when the air burned her lungs.

The hair on the back of her neck stood up—someone was breathing right behind her. She whipped around suddenly and was amazed to find herself looking up at a man who was impossibly tall, and just as impossibly wide. He wore a rusted suit of armor that covered thick muscles. His armor was chipped and dented, showing the many scars of battle. Old blood that had dried black speckled him everywhere.

Starlyn took a step back and tripped over the naked body of a dead young girl. Horrified, she pushed her way off the girl, who was the same age as herself, if not younger. The giant man towered over her, and she tried her best to meet his gaze. She did not succeed, realizing that there was nothing but black holes where his eyes should have been behind the dented visor.

"You have not been invited," he said in a booming voice which shook her bones.

Fear trembled through her core, yet she would not allow him to see this. Coming to her senses, she stood up and smoothed out her now blood-stained white dress.

"What do you want with Trust?"

The man stood up straighter in response to her tone and sudden change of demeanor.

"Trust from the House of Riyaadh? His soul belongs to me, and why is none of your concern."

He was not a wild beast like the other creatures that surrounded him. There was intelligence behind his words.

"Where am I?" she finally asked, unsure if she really wanted the answer. She took a step back when the man began to laugh.

"You have stepped yourself past the twelfth and final gate of hell. What do you think of my kingdom, girl?" He raised his arms and turned.

"This is where we go when we die? I was told it was beautiful ... peaceful," she said timidly, not wanting to believe that everyone was doomed to suffer.

The monstrous man stooped down so his face was aligned with hers. She found it uncomfortable being so close to a man with no eyes.

"The entire Underworld belongs to me, but this ... this is my home. It is true there are gates which are more pleasant places to visit, but my chosen come here. It was my will that brought these pitiful beings here. Some made bargains with me while others, well, let's just say they were not on my good side. I personally own every soul here. So, Starlyn DeTousan, what are you doing here?" He sneered.

He spoke to her as if she was a lost child and right now, she felt much the same way. She raised her chin in defiance despite her ignorance of where she was or even how she had gotten here.

"I am here to tell you that your kind, your … disciples are not welcome in my dreams. I won't tolerate you or any other demons there again."

She met the place where his eyes should be as she continued.

"As long as Trust is with me, I will protect him. If you think you will take him from me, I will show you how embarrassingly wrong you are."

Starlyn had no idea where her courage was coming from. Maybe she was protective of Trust because he had been the first person to be friendly toward her. It did not matter the reason; her words were quicker than her mind. She couldn't believe the foolishness of her tongue. He laughed again but this time he showed no amusement.

"How dare you threaten me. You do not even know who you protect. This is a game you cannot win, little girl. Now, if you are nice, I may send you home to your precious dreams. I do not think you wish to never wake up again. Or am I wrong to assume you do not want to spend eternity with me and my minions? If I am wrong and you wish to stay, then I will gladly find a place amongst the torture tables for you."

A sick smile lingered on his face.

"He is my friend," she stated boldly.

Before he responded, the air suddenly split open, revealing a large black gash in the fiery red sky. The giant growled angrily at the interruption. To Starlyn's complete amazement, a small boy stepped out from the tear in the sky and casually floated down to where they stood. The boy had to be about seven or eight and wore a plain brown robe. He smiled fondly at Starlyn, then turned to scowl at the giant.

"This has gone far enough. Belial, you know as well as any that the girl cannot be harmed," the boy said in a voice that did not fit his small form.

The monster named Belial grunted in disbelief.

"Enki, she is the one making threats in my domain, a domain that neither of you are welcome into. Her demands are absurd, to say the least. She may go free as law says, but Trust is mine."

The boy called Enki shook his head in return, obviously not happy with Belial.

"Do not be foolish. The fate of Trust is now intertwined with the Dawn Child's. He will not be harmed until she has passed on herself. You should know better than anyone the details of the contract. I cannot believe that you would even think of manipulating it to suit your wishes. We all realize what Trust has done in your kingdoms, but his involvement with the dawn child's future cannot be foreseen. It must be played out. You *will* wait."

She was missing some important detail, and she was not going to stand by without answers.

"Who's this dawn child and how am I involved?"

"I have said too much already, Starlyn, it is time to go." The boy spoke soothingly, instantly erasing the questions she had.

She suddenly had no idea what she was so worried about a moment ago. She took the boy's hand, feeling very lighthearted, and walked with him back through the hole in the sky without looking back. All around her there was blackness, but she was not afraid. It was unimaginable picturing herself ever being afraid again.

# Chapter Twenty

The homestead was uncommonly still. No birds sang, no children laughed, no wind blew through the trees. It was completely silent. The twin Seekers stayed their distance as they took in the area. It was never a good idea to walk into a situation that was unfamiliar, and nothing here seemed normal.

The farmstead itself was absolutely common. It consisted of a large two-story house, a barn, and a small pasture. It was not the place itself that made them wary. It was the silence that surrounded it—a dangerous kind of silence. None of the buildings were occupied by human or animal, though it appeared that they were used recently. Even though it was obvious that no one was here, they still used caution when they approached the house. Soft plums of white floated past their lips from the chilled air as they walked slowly through the empty yard.

Silently they entered the home, knowing exactly what they would find. Like the two other homes in the area that they had seen today, this one was in complete disarray. The shock had worn off after the first home, so seeing the furniture that was torn to pieces and strewn about the house did not bother them. They did not flinch at the sight of dried blood spattered across the walls and did not falter at the red streaks smeared on the floors. They had seen this all before.

They carefully stepped over the corn husk doll in the hallway and ignored the uneaten food still on the kitchen table. They came looking for life, but there were no survivors here to tell the tale of what happened. The large wolf tracks that were everywhere outside explained all that was needed to be known. Night Runners had visited the unsuspecting family that was living here and ended any future they had. The creatures were hungry and getting bored of waiting. It was a bold move to kill humans so close to *Hemel Deur*.

The Seekers concluded from the tracks outside that there had been only four in this raiding party. That was a smaller number than they had heard was in the area. They probably split the three houses between their numbers in order to feed the whole pack.

The brothers stood there silently, knowing that the threat was getting closer to the girl the Guardian escorted. The Mistress had sent her personal pack to find her, just like the Elders had sent their best. Jack-obee looked to his brother, who wore the same somber expression.

"This will be an interesting challenge for the Guardian."

His brother nodded in response, knowing that it was one that he would have to face by himself.

"He is strong. He will overcome them," Jack-obide said in return.

He must, or the girl would not survive long enough to fulfill her fate. If she did not, then they would all be lost, including themselves.

"He has much pride," his brother continued vaguely, but Jack-obide knew exactly what he was thinking of.

"She will show him the way. His future is in her hands just as much as hers is in his."

His brother nodded in agreement, understanding the fragile ties Starlyn and the Guardian had between them.

She had strength that was unknown even to herself, and she would need all of it. If only the Guardian knew what kind of change the girl would bring. Would he still have accepted the mission knowing the consequences? Most likely, he was very proud of his honor.

As for the brothers, well, they would do their duty also and relay the information about the Night Runners in the area, but it was not their fate to interfere. No, they could do nothing to help in this journey. They were here to observe and nothing more. Jack-obide stared a long time at the mismatched eyes of his brother, ever wondering when the time would come for their own part in history. For now they would wait and watch.

They left the farm exactly how they had found it, leaving no evidence that they had visited at all, not even a footprint. Soon they would reach the *Vellei Bosje* and plan out the next leg of the trek home to *Hemel Deur*. Until then, they would travel quick and silent. Strangers now would be scrutinized by everyone. No one would welcome the sight of the twins traveling on the roads with so much blood being spilt by the shapeshifters.

So they would save them the trouble and simply not be seen. It was the way of the Seeker, to be invisible unless needed. Jack-obee began to hum a sad song for the family that was no longer here. Jack-obide soon joined him as they walked away together, leaving the grim warning inside the house for others to see.

# Chapter Twenty-One

The next few days rolled by quickly and the closer they got to the trading post, the more questions Starlyn asked. The Guardian found himself becoming accustomed to her variety of interests and was beginning to enjoy his conversations with the girl. She had a way of seducing him into the discussion without realizing it. Her latest questions revolved around the vampire they had encountered days earlier.

"So do they really live off of human blood?"

Her smile seemed to never fade, even when the rains were heavy, like today. Her spirit was unstoppable.

"Demons feed on a variety of things. Some pain, others pleasure, but vampires feed on blood. It may be human or animal."

She chewed on this for a moment before coming up with her next question. He smiled to himself. He was sure she had several to choose from brewing in her head.

"So it was going to eat me then, or maybe my horse?"

"That is possible."

"Why didn't it try for you instead? You were closer."

"Maybe you looked tastier to him. My blood is probably not as sweet as yours."

He was unaccustomed to casual conversation, but somehow she had broken down his walls, and he began to speak to her with a familiar tone. It was never a good idea to get too close with the ones he escorted. It gave the wrong impression. The distraction of her being so friendly could ruin any advantage he may have by being alert. He reminded himself sharply to focus on the mission.

"How long before we reach *Vellei Bosje*?" she asked, suddenly changing the subject.

This was another trait he had come to expect from her. Her mind was scattered across a wide range of topics at all times. He found it was hard to pinpoint exactly what she wanted to know at times. But of course that did not matter. He had to stay professional with the girl.

"Not long, perhaps two days."

She glanced at him sideways. She was quick to catch on to his change in tone, and in turn changed hers.

"After that, how long until we reach our final destination?"

He paused briefly. "Four days."

She nodded, obviously lost in thoughts and not really listening to what the answer was.

"We do have one stop before *Hemel Deur*."

She was slightly ahead of him until he mentioned their destination, then she eased her mare back alongside him. It always put him on alert when she did that. She had a way of making very uncomfortable with her closeness.

"What's it like there? I've heard so much."

He wanted to tell her about the wonders of his home, but found himself reluctant. His duty was to get her to safety, not giving her more stories to fill her head.

So he kept his tone somber, trying to show that he did not wish to talk anymore. "You will see for yourself soon enough."

Her smile then turned into a scowl and he waited for her temper to be exposed. That was something else he had learned to expect from her. He sighed to himself and prepared for the inevitable.

"Why do you do that?" she asked in a low voice.

"Do what?"

Her face slowly turned red in frustration. "You know exactly what," she said curtly. "One minute you are friendly with me—you talk, joke, and I have even heard you laugh once. Then the next it is the same old short answers, always to the point and never opinionated. I hate it when you do that."

She was practically yelling by the time she was done, and he winced inwardly, knowing the truth of her words. He had never wanted to upset her, but he was finding himself distracted by her. That was a troubling problem.

When he failed to answer her, she put her heels into the mare and trotted several paces ahead, which was her version of pouting. This was a recurring cycle with her. They would get along fine, then fight, and then get along again. If his change in moods was shocking, how did she miss how extreme her own mood swings were? If he waited ten or fifteen minutes, she would be asking questions again. So that is exactly what he did. He waited.

While she stayed ahead of him for many miles, he sat thinking to himself. Maybe this time she was truly upset. Why did it bother him so much? Was he actually missing her constant questions? To his dismay, he also realized her pouting was working on him. He was actually feeling a little guilty for acting so rudely.

What was this girl doing to him? It was not until he finally decided that he would apologize did she finally reigned up again and continued in silence beside him. After a long and uncomfortable moment, she was the one to break the silence.

"I'm sorry, I just don't understand you. I think if we're stuck together, then we should at least be pleasant with each other. I don't know why you are afraid of being my friend, but you can't stop me from trying. You are just going to have to deal with it."

He continued his silence, not sure how to respond. Never before had someone he escorted made an effort to talk to him, to *know* him. Starlyn was the most complicated person he had met, simply because she was so simple. But his duty was simple also, and that was to concentrate on her safety, even if it bothered him that she thought he was afraid of something so trivial.

"I think that I can be pleasant," he said flatly.

He came to the conclusion that the conversation was over when she said no more. That was what he had wanted, wasn't it? Why did he still feel so guilty, then?

They moved forward toward the trading post and without making a scene, the Guardian again checked behind them. Something was following them, something that stayed in the shadows. Every time he tried to see it, the thing moved out of sight. Whatever it was, it did not seem hostile at the moment. He would have to deal with it until it presented an easier target to be rid of. Whatever it was, it had no idea what kind of trouble it just stepped into. He would enjoy discarding the annoying pest.

His main concern now was finding a place for them to stay for the night, which was fast approaching. Starlyn could have used a good warm bed, but that would not happen until they reached *Vellei Bosje*. So once again they found themselves sitting around a small fire under the shelter of the strange tarp. Their conversations had grown farther apart as the evening progressed, and eventually nothing broke the silence of the night except for the stormy winds that blew through their camp.

The wind had picked up a lot since they stopped for the night. Right now, it was fierce and unrelenting as it blew through the little depression he had found for them. They were both wet from traveling in the rain all day and now the uncommonly cold north wind cut to the bone. Regrettably they did not have any cover to block the wind and his tarp only barely protected them against the rain. It was not the most ideal place to stay, but he had found nowhere else within a reasonable range.

Despite the warmth of the fire, Starlyn began to shiver more and more. She huddled close to the fire in a ball of cloaks and blankets, trying to find some shelter from the wind. He was gritting his teeth at the feeling of helplessness as she froze. He hated not being able to provide what she needed right now.

He sat and brooded about it for a while and it was not long before he decided something had to be done, otherwise her health would be at stake. There was no practical solution to help her avoid the cold.

What if he sheltered her back and perhaps shared his body heat with her? The biggest obstacle in that plan was his worried thoughts. The words to suggest it were lost to him, and he raked his hand over his mask. He did not want her getting offended or to make her uncomfortable. Well, maybe he wanted to avoid being uncomfortable himself.

Her teeth began to chatter. His mind was fighting with the fact that he did not want to let himself get close to her, mentally or physically. But at the same time, it was his duty to protect her, even if it is the weather that was trying to hurt her. Finally, he stood and sat next to her with his back to the wind and rain. When she said nothing about his move, he rolled his eyes while reaching over and effortlessly lifted her in front of him. She stiffened at the gesture, but still said nothing. Eventually, she slowly stopped her shaking and relaxed more. Finally, after some time, she leaned back against him and fell asleep.

It was not until then did he relax, knowing that she would be fine and that the worst part was over with. He rested his chin on top of her head and closed his eyes, listening past the wind for anything out of the ordinary.

It must have been shortly after midnight when noises that did not belong in the night appeared. By now, the fire was burning low and he used his night vision to better take in the world around them. He did so without lifting his head and saw nothing, but that did not mean no one was there.

Distinct footsteps were coming closer. Soon the wind shifted slightly and he caught the strong odor of beer and urine. Being within a few days' ride of the trading post, he was not surprised by the appearance of men here. He cursed in his thoughts, realizing that he was not in the ideal position to deal with any possible threats. Starlyn was still asleep and was leaning heavily on his sword arm.

He listened closely at the steps and guessed that there were four of them. All were apparently drunk and trying to be quiet as they got closer. That was never a good sign.

"I see two of 'em sittin' there, boss," a man said in a low voice somewhere behind them. Another man not far off grunted in response.

"Three animals and a goodly amount of gear with 'em," a third said and another grunt in reply.

The men were beginning to get close now, their breathing heavy with excitement. It was then that Starlyn began to wake. She sighed softly and adjusted herself, causing the men to freeze. These men were on the prowl and had found what they thought were a couple of easy targets.

They were close enough, and he had to do something with the girl. He placed his palms on Starlyn's back and said a silent apology to her. He hated himself as soon as he thought of this plan, but there was no other option. With a hard shove, he sent her flying forward over the fire pit where he hoped she would land out of the way. In the same motion, he stood and drew the sword at his hip. He winced when Starlyn yelped as she hit the ground hard.

He quickly focused toward the men as he turned and faced the shocked attackers. He was satisfied as their faces turned white. They had just figured out they were about to rob a Guardian.

"Bloody Hell, he has one of those mask thingies on, boss!" one yelled as he ran into the darkness, leaving three.

The others stood their ground, looking back and forth between him and the girl.

"We can take him," the apparent boss said, and instantly one of the men lunged forward.

The thug was inexperienced with the sword he held; it was most likely stolen. His attempt to spear the Guardian was easily deflected to the side. Without pausing for the man to recover, he effortlessly slashed upward, cutting the man open from navel to neck. His mind was where it should be now. There were no distractions here. He was a killer at heart and it did not bother him when the man crumpled to the ground in pain.

The Guardian stepped over the screaming man to face the next oncoming attack. This man was able to hold his own for a moment, parrying the Guardian's swings, but he left himself open when he tried his own offensive strike. The Guardian's instincts were alert as the blood rushed through his heart and he went reflexively for the first opening. Not missing a moment, the Guardian slipped his blade into the man's side and up through his ribs into his heart. He wasted no time withdrawing the blade as the man fell beside his comrade.

Leaving both for dead, the Guardian turned to the final

man, whose face was now ashen. Was he having a change of heart? He quickly tossed down his own knife and backed away slowly with his hands in the air. The Guardian let him leave, knowing that he should kill the foul man to prevent him from preying on other travelers, but it was unnecessary. That was not his purpose.

He turned to find Starlyn staring at him with her hand covering her mouth. The blood drained from her face. She held a large stick she must have grabbed while he was fighting. He cursed to himself again. She should not have been subjected to this.

Before he could console her, she called out suddenly and lunged past him. She swung her stick as he dodged left just in time to strike the man who had run away. The thug crumpled to the ground, letting out a wail of pain. The man thrust his sword at Starlyn, but his aim was off. The Guardian easily blocked the blow, and with a smooth stroke, cut the man's throat.

Shocked, he turned to the girl. Why had she saved him? She stared at him, visibly shaking. Holding her makeshift weapon out in front of her. He approached her slowly and brushed aside the club. She dropped it and immediately started crying. He was shocked at his own reaction to her tears. He grabbed her and pulled her into a hug. She stayed there wordlessly crying for some time before he gently pushed her away.

She stood there as he squatted down and cleaned his blade on the man's shirt, then replaced it in its sheath. Ignoring the slight buzzing sensation from the sword at his back, he grabbed one of each man's feet and drug them far out of camp where he left them in the open.

The longer he was around the dead men, the hungrier the sword at his back became. Being so close to the blood filled him with the sudden urge to draw the broad sword. It gave him the urge to kill with it. He ignored it like he always did, but its hunger was strong today and it caused him to stop where he was. He did not like how close to camp he still was, but the sword wanted blood and being around it only made its effects on him worsen. A misstep with this particular blade would be disastrous. The sword would need to feed soon, but not now.

The Guardian reached into his cape and dropped the death coins onto the dirty bodies. The only remorse he had was that the girl had seen such violence. When he returned to camp, he found Starlyn still staring at the spot where the men had died.

He sighed to himself, not knowing what his next move would be, it pained him to think she was hurting. He walked to her and met her eyes. She said nothing, but the look on her face said it all. She was terrified of him.

"Are you alright? I did not mean to startle you, but it was necessary at the time." He tried to sound as calming as possible.

She glanced back toward the blood on the ground, and he understood that she was confused. It had happened so fast and she was left with nothing now but the gore of human remains.

"Those men would have killed me and done much worse to you," he said, plainly hoping she understood that he took the right course of action.

She finally nodded slowly to herself, and then crawled close to the horses, where she put her back against a small tree. She hugged her cape close around her while she pretended to sleep.

He sat contemplating what had happened and its effect on her. He would have to be more careful in the future. Averting his eyes, he knew it was his fault she was in this situation. He watched over her as she sat there, and he could tell by her breathing that she did not sleep much the rest of the night.

# Chapter Twenty-Two

Trust awoke and knew instantly that he was not alone. He raised his head from the bedroll on the ground and looked upon the familiar face of the Night Runner called Selene. She stood across from him, smiling smugly with her blue eyes reflecting the firelight, giving her a certain dangerous look he had not seen in her before. He had never met her in person, and seeing her clothed was a shock in itself. If you could call the sheer red dress that draped lazily on her body clothes. She had caught him completely off guard by showing up unannounced and in the flesh.

He sat up and took her in for a moment, trying to puzzle out why she was here and waiting for her to make the first move. He disliked how some people needed to be heard. He believed it was better to react to a situation, rather than to create it himself.

"Where's the girl?" she asked plainly, her smile immediately falling from her face.

She looked rather grumpy tonight—he would have to watch his tongue. Trust mentally went down the list of lies he could tell, knowing he had the advantage at the moment and he had no intention of losing it.

"I assume she is close. So far I have been following them toward *Vellei Bosje*, where I'm guessing they're going to arrive any time." He leaned back casually on one elbow and picked at a bit of dirt under his fingernail. "I thought with your special talents, you would've been tracking the girl yourself."

She looked at him a while longer, obviously not wanting to

tell too much. He had to admit it was curious the Night Runners were unable to locate her themselves. That was something he would have to remember.

She abruptly cocked her head to the left, toward the nighttime shadows. He lost his train of thought as he followed her line of sight, cursing himself when he saw the red-tinted reflection of eyes in the dark. He really should have expected there to be more than one. *Stupid*, he cursed himself. His odds of winning this round of their game were looking slimmer by the second.

Trust stood to face the newcomer, not liking his chances at escape or a fight while on the ground. The large man stepped into the firelight, and it took more effort than Trust would have liked to hold his composure. The man was shirtless and made of all muscle. He was taller than Trust, which he had noticed was uncommon in these parts. His blazing red eyes and white skin marked him as an albino.

His entire body, including his shaved head, was covered with strange black tattoos that swirled in an elegant way over the curves of his muscles. The soft lines they produced did not match the brute that wore them. He was terrifying to look at.

"Trust, may I introduce Gibbous," Selene said in an all too seductive voice.

Trust did not miss the fact she backed up a few steps, lowering her head slightly in the presence of this man. His mind reeled at the possibilities of this new player in this already strange game.

Judging by Selene's reaction, he was the alpha male of the pack. That was something he needed to remember as well. This man was dangerous and everything about him gave off a very primal feel.

With an unexpected lurch, Gibbous grabbed Trust by the

throat and threw him back against a nearby tree. Pain exploded from the back of his skull upon contact.

"Do not think we are ignorant, Necromancer. You know exactly where the girl is." The words came out of the man more like a growl than human speech.

Trust found himself having trouble looking the man in the eyes, not only from the blow to his head. He covered his own shock by laughing hoarsely.

"Do you think that I am afraid of death?"

The albino pressed his face closer to his ear. "I can do things to you which are far worse than death, little man." His breath was rancid in Trust's nose. "You will fear *me*!"

Trust squirmed under the pressure of the massive hand, trying to get a clear breath. He was going to lose consciousness soon.

"When the girl reaches *Vellei Bosje,* you will bring her to us," Gibbous demanded in a low breath.

"How do you expect me—she has a Guardian." He was getting lightheaded now.

"We will deal with the Guardian. You get the girl. I have heard that you can be very creative in the right circumstances. If you bring the girl, we will leave the sword for your efforts." The man finally released him.

Trust stood up straight and smoothed out his tunic, trying his best to cover his labored breathing with dignity.

Gibbous did not wait for an answer before he left the way he came, closely followed by Selene. Trust knew that the Night Runners expected obedience. That made it all the more fun to disobey them.

When he was sure the Night Runners had vanished into the night, he sat down by the fire. This game had decidedly gone on long enough. He warmed his hands mindlessly. They had gotten too close for his comfort, and he would have to figure out a way around this latest predicament.

It was not like him to allow another to push him around. He was obviously getting sloppy in his ways. How comfortable had he allowed himself to get living in *Groot Paleis*? Being surrounded by his very own army of spies and mercenaries had given him a false sense of security. It was now up to him to regain control of the situation. *How* was the real question. The last thing he needed was another question to add on to the already huge amount that he had.

Lost in thought, his eyes were unfocused as he stared into the flames dancing before him. He'd tried to contact Starlyn in her dreams twice since their first meeting with no success. That combined with the physical presence of the Night Runners was really beginning to irritate him. Luckily, his demon spy was doing its job beautifully.

He sighed and propped himself back on one elbow. Gibbous had been right when he said Trust knew exactly where the girl was. He would not have it any other way. Right now, they were only a day's ride from *Vellei Bosje.* What he would do with this information was a completely different story.

He hated the idea of helping the Night Runners after they threatened him. But then again, why would he help a girl he did not know? He finally came to the conclusion that if she was valuable enough for the Night Runners to track down and have a Guardian Elite escorting her, then maybe she was worth his time. Wide awake now, he decided perhaps he would try to find her dreams again.

It took him almost an hour to properly draw the protective runes around his chosen space this time. Traveling to the underworld would leave the body you left behind vulnerable, and being out in the open made it doubly dangerous. The runes he drew had to be perfect; if one mistake was made, an attacker could easily destroy his body. With the Night Runners so close, that was not an option. When the runes were drawn right, only someone of great skill could get close to him.

Finally done, he sat himself in the circle he had drawn and closed his eyes. He decided the safest place to start was inside the first gate. The transition was easy and he opened his eyes in another world. The dense wall of fog immediately put him at ease. This was home for him; among the dead was where he could really feel alive again.

It was unlikely he would encounter any threats surrounded by the mist; only confused souls wandered at the first gate. Satisfied he was not in danger, he took his trusted flute from his belt. With a deep breath, he played a song of finding and infused it with the song that was whispered in Starlyn's soul.

Every living creature had its own song. Each song could be used to control, manipulate, and eventually even destroy the person. He tried not to concentrate on that as he played; the trick would be useless if he lost focus. Instead, he imagined her smile and honest laugh. The pitches became higher as he played. Her soul song was remarkably sweet and happy, full of wonder for the world around her. As he played, his own soul seemed to relax, and he closed his eyes, enjoying the private moment.

He had been expecting disappointment again, so when he received the first vibrations of a response, he smiled to himself. He let the finding song work its way through the shadows and eventually draw a map in his mind. Satisfaction radiated from him. This little trick was not easy to master and was near impossible without knowing her soul song.

Once again, he found himself walking through pure darkness, but this time he had an idea what to expect from her dreams. When he emerged from the dark, he found himself in the sunlit field. The sky was full of white fluffy clouds that floated across the sky at surreal speeds. If he focused on them too long, he was sure to get dizzy. Dreams were always so odd, he mused.

He walked on and soon stumbled upon a massive stone structure sitting alone in the middle of the grass. Curious, he walked completely around it and found no entrance. He placed his palm against the warm stone and could feel her presence inside. She obviously wanted to feel secure and he hated to do this to her safe house, but his time was running short. Placing his other hand on the wall, he began to push. He pushed with all his strength and soon the bricks began to move inward. He smiled and threw his shoulder into the wall. The bricks reformed quickly behind him, making him feel like he was being swallowed by the structure.

Trying to avoid panic, he continued to push, eventually falling to the ground alongside the debris. He locked eyes with the girl inside, who was sitting with her back to the far wall, knees pressed close to her chest. He greeted her with a reassuring smile.

"Starlyn DeTousan," he said with a bow. "Please forgive my intrusion, but I have been trying to reach you for some time now."

Her face washed with confusion, fear, then recognition. He coughed slightly as the dust settled at their feet.

"How'd you do that?" she asked.

"I can do much more than that, my dear. Sometime I will tell you the full story, but for now my time is limited. Those fellows from before will find me here far too soon for my liking."

To his disbelief, she shook her head and beamed at him. "They won't bother you. I talked with Belial and he said he would leave you alone."

It was his turn to look shocked. His first instinct was to laugh, but when he looked at her face, he decided against it.

"How is that possible...? Starlyn, tell me everything."

She nodded in agreement and motioned to a set of chairs that were not there before. She was indeed powerful and definitely in control of her safe house.

"I followed one of those creatures and I ended up with Belial. Let me tell you, he is not the nicest person to be around." She shrugged like she was speaking of a grumpy old man down the road. "I told him to leave you alone. He laughed at me, of course. Then a boy showed up—Enki ... I think, and told Belial he couldn't touch you."

The more she talked, the more he realized that she had really done these things. She had stood in front of the ruler of the underworld and lived to talk about it.

"Why?" he asked simply, his confusion growing.

"You believe me!" She smiled triumphantly. "Enki said your fate was intertwined with some Dawn Child and while that person still lived, Belial couldn't lay a hand on you."

Trust stared at her blankly. He had come for answers and only received more questions. Now he had to figure out who in the hells was this Dawn Child and how his life was involved. It was apparent by her smiling face she had no idea what she had witnessed, only that she had done her part to keep him safe within her dreams. Maybe she was not hiding anything after all.

"Why does Belial want your soul?" she asked suddenly.

He was reluctant to elaborate on the subject and began to think of ways around this conversation.

"I figure you owe me this for helping you. It can't be too much to ask for honesty?" She spoke plainly. "Trust, how'd you get here? How'd you knock down my walls?"

She was right, of course. If her story was true, he owed her a great debt, but he knew what he told her may only endanger her more.

"Starlyn, there's no simple answer to any of those questions, but I will try to explain the best that I can." He brushed off dust from his jacket while he spoke. "When I was a boy, much younger than you, I discovered that I could travel to a different world than the one we live in. Even different from the one we're sitting in now." He found himself hesitant to continue, but pushed on. "I explored this world with a hunger to know everything. This new world I found felt right to me—this world was home to me."

She nodded, keeping quiet for the moment.

"Starlyn, to be blunt, I am a Necromancer. That world of mine is the Underworld … the land of the dead."

He watched her eyes for a reaction but found none that he could decipher.

"In my travels beyond the gates of hell, I discovered I had a talent. One most necromancers do not possess. I could create things; I could change things. These new skills made me untouchable in the underworld. No demon could come near me and no gate could hold me."

His explanation left much out, but letting her know more would put him at risk. He had secrets upon secrets and some things were better left for another time.

"I was young, and power made me reckless. One day, I found myself cornered by many powerful demons. My foolishness had finally done me in—or so I thought."

He turned from her then, hiding the pain he felt when remembering the moment.

"I was rescued by a creature who was forbidden to intervene. The laws put down by the old gods do not allow for demons to assist necromancers. After that, we became comrades. The laws did not stop us from exploring the extent of my abilities together. This angered Belial more than any other mortal soul had ever done before."

She still sat, not flinching at any of this and not saying anything in return. It had been a very long time since he had told anyone so much of his life. He did not know why, but he knew she would keep his secrets safe with her.

"So, after a small scuffle with some of his minions, I ended up destroying a part of the tenth gate. That and the discovery of my friendship with the higher demon angered him so much he swore my eternal soul would be his. If I am ever captured by him, my days behind the twelfth gate will be very painful," he said lightly, trying to sound more upbeat than he was.

He gave Starlyn a moment to think about the information he had given her.

"So you were hunted for your own foolishness and broke down my wall because you have the ability to create and destroy. I get that, but how did you come here? My dreams?"

He chewed on this for a moment, trying to find the easiest way to explain.

"Dreams lay near to death. Sometimes when people die in their sleep, they simply got lost beyond the gates, and sometimes when you wake from a dream in which you were dead, you really were."

She had taken all this information with such stride that he began to wonder if this kind of knowledge was something she already knew.

"Who's Enki?" she asked in the same calm tone she'd had this whole conversation.

"Enki and Belial both are old gods. Enki is the keeper of divine law, while Belial is the keeper of the underworld. Not many people get the honor to meet any of the old gods and meeting two is even more unheard of." He did not have to hide how impressed he was.

Not many knew that the old gods still existed in a world unreachable by humans. He had tried himself to reach their world with no success.

"They are not the first ones," she said, almost in a whisper.

He stood, then crouched in front of her, meeting her sad grey eyes. There he saw something that was not meant to be there. Something that was much older than the girl that sat before him. Who was this girl?

"I have told my story. Now tell me what you are talking about." It came out harsher than he would have liked.

She sighed softly to herself. "I don't know where to start. Let's see—I have had dreams since I can remember. Not normal everyday dreams, but something ... different." Her eyes became distant. "Sometimes in those dreams I can hear voices. Sometimes they speak directly to me; sometimes they speak to each other."

He held his composure the best he could, but hearing that this girl talked to the old gods on a regular basis was more than he could have hoped for. She may have just explained why she was so important to the Mistress. Before he could come to any conclusions, though, he would have to research it more.

"My dear girl, do you have any idea why you are going to see the Elders?"

The question seemed to catch her completely off guard.

"No." She sounded as if she was far away, then her face began to fade.

Recognizing the danger he was suddenly in, he reached for his flute.

"Starlyn, you are waking up now and if I stay, my soul will be lost. I will speak to you again soon," he said quickly as the walls around them became more and more transparent. With a quick tune from his flute, he returned to his body.

The sun still had a long way to go before it would rise, but he would not sleep tonight. He needed to find out more about Starlyn, and more importantly, about this Dawn Child that had apparently saved his soul.

# Chapter Twenty-Three

The morning was surprisingly sunny and it was a relief to be without the rain. Despite her weariness, Starlyn was cheered some by the warmth the daylight produced. She helped pack up camp even though the Guardian kept insisting that she sleep more. She tried to appreciate his concern, trying her hardest not to lose her temper because he thought her too breakable.

He meant well, but she wanted to be as far away from this place as possible. Every time she turned around, she saw the blood that stained the ground out of the corner of her eye. It unnerved her to be so close to such a death. It was one thing to hear stories about highwaymen attacking. It was a whole other thing to witness it. Death was not something to take lightly, no matter how much the men deserved it.

She did not want to admit it, but try as she might, she could not deny that she looked at the Guardian differently now. Killing was obviously something that came naturally to the man, and that suddenly made her rethink everything she thought she knew about him. He had killed to protect her, but did that make a difference? She was not sure if it was the killing that rattled her or the way it was carried out. He had no remorse for what had happened, no emotion at all. She pushed the thoughts from her mind, focusing on the fact that he had indeed saved her and that she would try to be grateful for that.

When camp was packed, she refused his offering of dried berries and oats, saying honestly that she was not hungry. That did not stop him from offering them again. She reminded herself to be grateful, not annoyed. It was not until they mounted again and headed down the road did she begin to finally relax a bit. As they rode, she realized the two of them were right back where they started: strangers.

She felt like he was a different person now. They had been riding together for a week and she knew nothing about the man beside her. *That's not true*, she thought to herself, *I've just learned something new.* He was a killer. Duty bound, ruthless, and loyal. She was seeing him now, the real him.

Coming to terms with this was a bigger challenge than she had expected. To her, he was kind and gentle, but to the world around them, he was a Guardian.

They rode in silence for a long time, both seemingly engrossed in their own thoughts.

"I am sorry for making you bear witness to the death of those men." Her jaw fell slack. "You should not have been subjected to such violence." He looked to the ground when he spoke, avoiding eye contact.

It warmed her heart despite her earlier musings. Maybe he was not as callous as she'd previously assumed.

"You lost this at camp." He held out her stone necklace that was gifted from Trust.

"Thank you."

After everything that had happened to her, she had to admit she liked being here. She enjoyed the thought that she was actually a *somebody*, at least for the moment. It was straight out of a fairy tale! Her, Starlyn DeTousan, a sheepherder turned lady with her brave knight beside her.

Smiling to herself, she redirected her attention to her knight. She wanted to know the man under the mask so much. He had saved her life twice and she would find a way to repay him for that. It did not matter that he was ordered to do it. She found it hard to believe he was ordered to keep her warm, like he did last night. Her heart picked up a beat or two when she thought about it, and she turned away from him to hide how red her face was becoming.

He was so confusing; one minute he was all business, ready to kill to protect her, and the next he would be helping her tend her wounds or practically feeding her. Remembering all of that made her face turn even redder than before.

The clear, crisp day made the ride more enjoyable than she had hoped for. They had been traveling alongside the *Bloed Hout* for some time now, and she found herself staring into the deep woods with a dreamy eye. It was an amazingly beautiful place, with the red leaves shining brightly in the sun. A wonderful earthy smell blew past them on the wind, making her want to ride through those woods and explore their depths. Looking so closely at them now, she could not fathom why they were feared so much. She thought the woods were wonderful.

"I can't figure out what is so scary about the *Bloed Hout,*" she said, almost to herself.

"*De Oudsten* have had control of the woods for thousands of years. It is their presence that the people fear."

The Guardian's response surprised her out of her mindless wanderings.

She had not realized he was paying attention to her. She steered her mount closer to his so she could have a proper conversation.

"Why are they feared so much? If you represent any part of them, then there's nothing about them I fear."

He turned his head slightly away from her, perhaps because of her compliment. Seeing his almost shy reaction to her flattering remark made her more determined to find a way to get him to open up.

"People fear what they do not understand," he stated, then pointed in front of them. She followed his finger but could not decipher what he was looking at. "The mountains there, they are called *Aarde Beenderen* or Earth Bones."

She recognized the name. It seemed so strange to actually be seeing them herself. Even though they were fairly close to her home, she'd never imagined traveling here. The Guardian then pointed to the right, past the red treetops.

"The tallest peak," he continued. "That's called *Trap Aan Hemel* or Stairway to Heaven. That is where we are going. That is where *Hemel Deur* lies."

She looked upon the mountain with awe. It was huge, much larger than the rest of the mountains beside it. It still seemed so unreal that she was here. How would they ever get to the top of that?

"What does *Hemel Deur* mean?"

"It means Heaven's Door. That is my home."

Hearing this made Starlyn think of her own home. She missed her family so much. She even missed the mule that pulled the cart. She peered at the Guardian riding beside her and wondered what the word home really meant to him. Did he have family that waited for him? A wife, perhaps?

"How long before we get all the way up there?" she asked, trying to get away from the subject of home.

"Four, maybe five days. We will be stopping in *Bos Vlucht* for a day before we reach our final destination."

She nodded to herself

The road seemed empty today. They'd passed a few homes, but had seen no one around. They were coming upon yet another seemingly empty home and Starlyn took the time to examine it closer. The curtains in the windows were pulled back and there was no movement inside. The front door was slightly open and banged quietly against the frame. She came to the conclusion that they were indeed empty. Her mind quickly searched for an explanation so that she wouldn't have to ask any more silly questions. Hard as she tried, she came up with none.

"Where are all of the people?" she finally said while chewing on her lower lip.

He glanced to the house and sighed to himself, obviously not wanting to have this conversation.

"The rumors of the *Nacht Agenten* have scared the people here. Either they have boarded themselves inside the houses or they have traveled to *Vellei Bosje* for safety." He seemed to overstate the fact that they were rumors, making her heart beat quicker. She stared back to the empty house and wondered what the family that lived there was doing right now. Being so close to the red-topped trees beside them was a little less comfortable. She shivered.

To her relief, in the distance she began to notice the streaming lines of smoke from chimneys. She knew that meant life was still close enough to give her a relatively safe feeling. Before long, the outline of the trading post formed in the distance. Its walls were not nearly as impressive compared to *Groot Paleis*, but this was something entirely different. The wall that was visible from outside was constructed from large trees. Bare of branches, they lined the entire town that created the trading post. She could smell signs of life everywhere now. Wood smoke, horses, decay.

"That's *Vellei Bosje*, right?" She stood up in her saddle to better see, but was a bit disappointed when his only response was to nod. He seemed to be done with conversation. She glanced back at him and watched his gaze dart from one side of the road to another. The way he was riding had changed too. He rode not just straighter but almost on his toes, as if ready to strike at any minute.

"What is it? What's wrong?" she asked, suddenly worried.

His eyes flicked behind them before he met her gaze. Then he visibly relaxed.

"Nothing. Something just caught my attention." He regained his composure perfectly and faced forward again.

Starlyn was not quite convinced, though. She too began to subtly look around, trying to see what exactly caught his attention. All she saw was the dusty road in front of them, surrounded by too quiet homesteads. She shivered at the emptiness of it all. Night Runners? She could not think of anything much more frightening.

Her anticipation grew as they got closer to the trading post, and a new sense of excitement filled her. They were getting so close to their destination that she could almost picture herself already on her way home. Only a few more weeks and everything would be back to normal. With that thought, she began to hum a little tune. She could not remember where she had heard it before, but she knew that she liked it.

*Vellei Bosje* was unlike anything she had ever seen before. Once closer to the trading post, she saw one side of the structure was a river that flowed toward the woods next to it and like the woods it was a deep red color that reminded Starlyn of darker things. She trembled, thinking back to the man she had helped kill.

The *Bloed Hout* itself provided a sort of shelter on another side, and the city was built on the crest of a steep incline, protecting it from intruders on all sides.

She recalled her father telling her the outpost had outgrown its wall and horses were not allowed within the streets of the town. The stables in which they put their animals bordered along the outside walls and they had a sort of storage unit you could rent to put some of your belongings in so you did not have to carry much. She did not have many things that belonged to her, but she did not like the idea of someone else going through her stuff. The Guardian shrugged off her protest, and they proceeded into the outpost.

They traveled on foot, heading toward an inn where they were to meet with Jack-obee and Jack-obide. Despite her protests, the Guardian carried the supplies they needed with them on his back, including her pack, and she could not hide her irritation. He had a way of making her feel useless that really annoyed her.

As they walked, she took in the scenes around her. From what she could see, there were buildings spread out throughout the area and a lot of smaller warehouses. The main streets were covered with small shops that held a variety of goods made to entice a traveler. If she could spend the day wandering here, she would still not see everything that was on offer. As they weaved through the crowds of people, she glanced down streets, distracted by the loud-mouthed merchants telling of their wares.

When they passed a man selling meat pies, her mouth began to water. The aroma was amazing! She remembered that she had not eaten today. Giving her companion her best puppy dog eyes, she slowed her pace to a crawl. He noticed immediately that she was falling behind and turned around to see what she was doing. Knowing she finally had his attention, she turned back to the stand where the man had also noticed her interest. His calls got louder as he tried to convince her to come closer.

She looked again at the Guardian and gave him what she thought was her best smile. Shoulders sagging a little, he sighed then nodded toward the vendor. She let out a little squeal of delight and rushed to the man. She wasted no time biting into the flaky pastry. Satisfaction bloomed as the juices ran down the corner of her mount. It was fresh and she burnt her tongue as she shoved the remainder into her mouth. She instantly regretted only getting one and peered back longingly as they continued on.

The walk to the Merchant's Inn was shorter than she'd thought it would be. The inn was huge compared to Cat's Cradle. This one had to be three stories tall, and the outside was finely decorated with small shrubs beside the door and flower boxes under the windows. The shutters were a bright red that stood out beautifully against the stone exterior. To top it off, the smell coming from the direction of the kitchen made her mouth water.

As she waited for the Guardian to arrange their room, she took her time taking in the surroundings, but made sure she didn't stray far from his side. She peeked into the common room and found it was mostly empty. There were a couple of men sitting in a corner with some wine next to them. They played an unfamiliar stone game on the table that made her wish she was closer to see. While she thought about sneaking closer, a firm hand on her shoulder startled her, making her yelp. Distracted by the game, she hadn't seen the Guardian walk up behind her.

"Don't do that!" she said, a bit fluttery.

His eyes were apologetic as he motioned toward the stairs nearby. With a glance back, she confirmed that the two men were now staring at her, so she hurried to get to her room. To her utter disappointment, their room was on the third floor of the inn and the stairs were enough to get her almost wheezing by the time she reached the top. When they entered the room, she was grateful that it had a window this time. She immediately ran to the rather large bed and jumped on top of it. She was pleasantly surprised at the softness of it. This was the nicest room she'd ever been able to stay in.

Like a giddy little girl again, she jumped off the bed and raced into the adjoining room to find the oddest-looking wash tub she had ever seen. It was steel, which was rare anyways, but this one also had what seemed to be a small stove under it. She giggled to herself when she realized it was indeed a stove that was already lit and the tub was filled with water.

She'd hurried out of the room to get a fresh pair of clothes when she caught a glimpse of herself in the large mirror. She stared for a while, trying to absorb the fact that the reflection was her own. She was a mess, that was for sure. Her hair was raggedly thrown up into her usual bun and her eyes were rimmed with dark circles, not to mention the dirt that was streaked across her chin. After she successfully retrieved her clothes, she hurried back to the tub.

It took her no time at all to strip down and step into the bath. The water was so hot it made her suck in her breath as she sat down. This being the first time she had had a hot bath, she would not complain. She settled in finally and began to relax as she grew accustomed to the water. She splashed water over her shoulders and found the bruising on her arm was fading nicely. She was not sure how long she sat in the tub, but when her eyelids began closing, she knew it was time to get dressed.

She dressed quickly in the clothes the Guardian asked her uncle to make for her. The cream tunic draped over her wonderfully and she remembered why she liked this ensemble so much. She found the dark blue riding skirt made the outfit look very elegant, even though it was plain, and the material made it feel a little too expensive for her. All in all, it did make her look very nice in the mirror. She decided she would leave her hair down for the moment and give it a chance to breathe. Before she left the room, she made sure that the necklace the Trust had given her was securely in place. The blue of the skirt made the hue of the stone seem bluer somehow, and she liked how it complemented her eyes.

She wandered out of the room humming the strange tune to herself, and was greeted by the now familiar eyes of the

Guardian on her. She could not explain it, but his gaze made her heart beat a little faster. When he looked away from her in his usual oddly shy way, she could not hold back her smile. As she opened her mouth to say something she was sure to regret, she was interrupted by someone knocking on the door. The Guardian cracked the door open and was greeted by the twins.

"We have arrived." She did not know which was which, but she was almost positive it was Jack-obide who spoke. "And we have news that is very interesting."

He eyed Starlyn out of the corner of his eye. The other brother was not nearly as subtle as he grinned at her. The Guardian obviously saw the question behind their gaze and nodded for them to continue. Jack-obide, or who she thought was Jack-obide, turned to her suddenly and held up a pair of boots.

"Your mother would like to wish you a very happy coming of age celebration." He spoke in an upbeat tone that she was sure was meant to cheer her up.

"She is sorry that you cannot celebrate the proper way, but hopes these will be useful to you on your journey," the other brother finished.

She glanced at the Guardian and watched his eyes for a reaction while her face began to burn. *They did not have to announce it to the whole world*, she thought bitterly. She snatched the boots from them, a little more aggressive than necessary, and went to sit on the bed with her back to the three of them.

Seeing those boots made her heart ache. She missed her mother so much and now the day had arrived that they were both looking forward to. The only thing she had now was this very practical gift from her very practical mother and that could hardly be considered a celebration. She tried her hardest to hold back the tears that were threatening the edges of her eyes.

This day was supposed to make her happy. It was supposed to help her decide the course of her life, but right now the whole coming of age thing seemed like a joke as she sat in a strange room full of even stranger people. She was exhausted and let a few tears slip from her eyes. Would she ever see home again?

# Chapter Twenty-Four

It was clear from Starlyn's breathing that she had fallen asleep finally. The Guardian had worried the whole ride here that she would fall asleep atop her horse and was grateful she was resting now.

He had been more worried about her reaction to the violence last night. He thought about it over and over again, but found that his reaction was correct for the situation. The thieves had the opportunity to leave once they had been discovered, yet they chose to stay and fight a Beschermer. It was no secret that *De Oudsten* made sure that all *De Beschermer* were trained in warfare from a very young age, but that did not stop the greedy men. He came to the conclusion that there was no way around exposing her to the violence. If it was ever possible to have spared her, he would have without question. He did not want to be the one that ruined her innocent outlook on life and he would continue to try to protect her from the violent way of the world. This would include protecting her from his own violent way of life.

The twins had told him nothing he did not already know. This included that it would take about two days to reach the farmstead called *Bos Vlucht*. Of course, he knew the place very well. It was a regular stop for him. Besides, it was his duty to present the girl to all of *De Oudsten*. He'd assumed originally that would include the farm in the middle of the *Bloed Hout*. That meant he had only a few days left with the girl. He had no idea why that information was so disconcerting. She would be safe from all threats as long as she was within the walls of his home, and that was all that mattered right now.

He pondered the information. Did they say coming of age? He had not realized the girl was so young. Her eyes seemed filled with age.

She was upset but she tried to hide it. If he remembered correctly, this was a significant occasion amongst the common people. It pained him to see her so sad after she had overcome so much on this trip.

This kind of feeling was out of place. It was obvious the *Nacht Agenten* being so near had sent his emotions out of control. He had trouble focusing knowing they were so close. That was the only explanation for his lapse in resolve. He knew that no matter how much he wanted to make her feel better, he had to focus on the more pressing matters he had to attend to right now.

The scent of the *Nacht Agenten* was everywhere in the town, throwing off his senses. His nerves were raw and his muscles tense, a reaction he had never had before when facing a threat. Then again, Iridium may have been right when he said that they were something he was not familiar with. It was so strange having something so familiar be so new at the same time. That was the only way he could describe it.

His reactions now seemed to be instinctual, and that was something he had tried to suppress almost his whole life. It did not matter really what the cause was, only that this was a dangerous situation for him to put Starlyn in. If his mind was not sharp, then he would be useless to her.

It was still early in the day; they had made surprisingly good time. He briefly watched Starlyn as she mumbled to herself softly. Maybe he should pack the girl up and leave right now. He glanced down at her face and knew that was not what she needed right now, but at the same time it was exactly what he had to do to keep her safe. He could let her sleep a while longer while he went to get some supplies that they needed. He would leave *De Zoekers* here to watch her so he knew she would be safe. The time away would also give him the opportunity to try to unravel what his nose was telling him, and maybe even track one or two of the creatures down in the process. That would give him a few less threats to worry about later.

He left her there in the safe hands of Jack-obee and Jack-obide, yet noticed how much he did not want to. Right now, in order to be useful to the girl, he would have to figure out what was going on with his emotions first and that was the most important thing. He wandered the streets, only half paying attention when he was ordering the supplies he needed. They all agreed to have the things waiting for him with his horses, which he also made sure were packed up and ready to travel. The errands he ran did not take long, but the sun was beginning to fall now.

As he walked back toward the inn, he came across a scent that made the hair on the back of his neck stand up. Instinctually, a low growl slipped out of his throat and startled a passing man. With the smell came the same sort of images he had been seeing all day. Flashes of pictures in his mind, but nothing made sense to him. He was sure it had something to do with the scent.

This scent was fresh. Was that why the images were so clear? He inhaled again and determined three wolves had gone this way. Two males and one female. Another breath and more images flashed past him. A lone wolf stalking his prey in the night, making no sound while he hunted. He could feel the wolf's hunger and confidence.

The image was as clear as what it meant. It was more than a picture; it was a name and this male was named Silent Hunter. Being raised among humans, he had no idea how to process what was happening. He took another step in the direction they went, and took another breath.

The next image he caught made him stop in the street, suddenly blind to the world around him. He was surrounded by a black landscape and an empty sky. The night scene made something deep within him excited by the possibilities that hid in that blackness. The female was called Starless Night.

He kept walking. The scent was indeed fresh, and he found himself swept up in the moment of discovery. He was enjoying this hunt more than *De Oudsten* would have allowed, more than he should have allowed himself. It was dangerous to let this side of him run free.

He turned the corner and was greeted by a new scent, which made him growl deep from his chest. The hairs on his neck rose.

He clearly saw a moon that was more than half, but less than full. The last male was named Gibbous, and he had something the other two did not.

He took another deep breath, trying to decipher it. His smell was infinitely unique; it told the Guardian that Gibbous was in charge. He was powerful, fierce, and he was a threat.

Gibbous was the alpha of the pack, and the unspoken warning that followed his scent was enough to make the Guardian's mouth water. He wanted to kill this one and had no idea why his body was reacting in such a way. It did not matter —he knew this was the time to kill these creatures, before they could get anywhere near the girl. He must satisfy this primal need for dominance.

He followed them closely, almost recklessly. His senses were becoming more and more alive with every step that he neared them.

The Guardian focused himself, remembering to control his instincts. He slowed down, eventually realizing he was going into an area of the town that was deserted. He peered at the sky.

It was dark now and a thick fog had begun to settle over the trading post. He had been distracted too long and was nowhere near the inn.

"Damn it!" he roared to himself.

Starlyn was in danger, he was sure of it now. They had kept him busy following a false trail. They had guessed that he was weak when dealing with a pack and played on his weakness to lure him away.

An image of the sleeping girl flashed through his mind, sending a jolt of adrenaline through his body, and he began to run. As he ran, he could feel others following him. They had been watching him the whole time. He gritted his teeth to hold back the irritation. They were not important now, only the girl was. As if to solidify his fears, he heard a nearby howl break through the silent night. The first was joined by another one farther away.

"Shit," he said between clenched teeth.

They knew he was coming, but that would not stop him. He had a few tricks they were not aware of as well. He smiled to himself, knowing that this hunt was just beginning.

# Chapter Twenty-Five

Trust had no idea when he'd made his decision, but it was too late to turn back now. One thing he did know was that if he was going to pull this off, he would have to act quickly so the Night Runners would not suspect his change of plans. For now, he would let them think he was playing their game, but it would not take them long to find out he had deviated from the rules. Like Gibbous had stated the night before, they were not ignorant brutes as some people thought.

His window of opportunity was short and he knew the girl would not be alone for long, if at all. He found himself standing before the Merchant's Inn without realizing how he had gotten there. His thoughts were so jumbled he had not noticed where he was going. Standing there in the dark and empty street, he suddenly knew his choice to not let the Night Runners or the Elders have her was the right one.

She was valuable, and until he knew exactly what she could do, he would need to stay close. Her unique talents would need to be cultivated, and he thought of himself as a good teacher. Besides, he would not let the wolves think they could push him around. He was Trust from the House of Riyaadh after all, a necromancer, and not someone to be toyed with.

Now he would have to find the best way to get the girl alone. Once alone, he knew he could convince her to leave with him. How he would accomplish the first task was beyond him at the moment. It was not like him to go into any situation blind, but right now time was not on his side.

He would need to come up with some more information

on who was in the room with her and quickly. His demon spy had already informed him exactly what room she was in, but failed to notice if anyone else was with her. That was one downfall of those kinds of enchantments. They gave the demon tunnel vision. Right now, the little monster only had eyes for one person and that was Starlyn.

With a deep breath, he ignored the nagging feeling in the back of his head telling him he was running out of time, and went inside. He found the common room nearly empty. The only man there was far into his cup and beginning to fall asleep at the table. He did not really think this room was full of information, but then he noticed the wait staff was still busy cleaning and thought again. The workers at places like this knew everything that there was to know about their patrons.

The two who were working right now were both women, and that was a lucky break. He put on his most dazzling smile and took a seat. The older of the two came and took his order, but completely ignored his efforts of charm. He took a drink of his wine and continued telling himself that the solution would present itself soon. Sure enough, not halfway through his cup, the women began to talk while they worked. He did not have to wait long before the subject turned to a familiar sounding girl.

"That pretty little thing seemed a little too relaxed with 'em," the older woman said, sympathy thick in her voice.

"It ain't natural, that's for sure," the second one responded in a casual tone. "If I were surrounded by those strange folks, I wouldn't be happy."

There was a slight pause as they collected a few plates and wiped off the tables.

"Well, that Guardian fellow left a goodly time ago, so now she's only with those twins." The younger girl did not seem to be bothered by the situation.

It was not that odd to see a Guardian this close to the *Bloed Hout*, but the older one seemed concerned by their presence.

"Yeah, but those two are certainly different. Who ever saw a man with one green eye and one blue? That poor girl can't be more than seventeen cycles. She should be at home with her mom, lookin' for a man to take care of 'er," the older one continued, not willing to let it go.

"Those two I wouldn't mind, but the one with the mask gives me the jeebies. Besides,

maybe one of 'em is her man."

The older woman's jaw dropped open in shock.

"I bet the trollop is shackin' up with the lot of 'em," a man from the kitchen chimed in.

The younger woman laughed with him and walked out of the common room.

"Bloody hells, old Dodger is asleep in his beer again," the older one said, following her

out.

Trust smiled to himself; now he knew exactly what he was up against. Thank the gods for gossip. The two men the women talked about fit the description of the twin Seekers from *Groot Paleis*. Knowing this, he headed upstairs to the rooms. Gossip could not always be trusted and he was not leaving anything to chance.

He quietly walked past the room Starlyn occupied, making it seem like he was going further down the hall. Once a good distance away, he slowly crept back to her room. Pulling out a small shard of mirror, he quickly dropped to the floor and slid it under the door.

Moving the mirror slightly, it reflected the entire room for him. Starlyn was asleep on the bed, and sure enough, the twin seekers sat playing cards at the table. Silently, he retrieved his mirror and tip-toed back downstairs.

Seekers would be much easier to deal with than the Guardian. He was the dangerous one. Since they were twins, their songs would be very similar, maybe even the same. His job just became a little easier.

He set a silver coin on the table before he left. It was much more than the wine was worth, but the information he had gotten was priceless.

Once outside, he checked the street, making sure no one was around. A thick fog had settled on the trading post, giving it a very unnatural atmosphere. The streets were completely deserted. It seemed the rumors of the Night Runners were keeping everyone indoors. He pulled out his flute and took in its simple design. When his mysterious friendship with the demon began and he had given the flute to him, the demon had told him he was destined for great things in the underworld and above. He wondered if the Dawn Child had anything to do with that or if it was just an idle compliment.

Focusing on the room Starlyn and the Seekers were in, he closed his eyes and listened to the world around him. He carefully probed into the room and found the spy he had placed there. With little effort, he tapped into the consciousness of the demon. He listened around the room and found Starlyn's song easily enough. Then he searched for the other ones. Just like he imagined, the brothers' songs were identical. He smiled to himself, then began to play.

He could not waste any time here, so he played his own version of a lullaby, hoping the trick would work. He knew the Elders had men and women that gave their sleep and food to these people, but the mind was a complex thing. He would trick them into sleeping and it would be a very deep sleep. After a time, he decided it was now or never and changed his tune to the one that represented Starlyn. He played for a long time before a familiar shadow appeared in the window above. Her hair cascaded over her shoulders and was rumpled like she had just woken up. She waved absent mindedly toward him, a smile creeping across her face.

Putting his flute away, he waved to her to come down. He watched, holding his breath as she peered behind her, then back to him. Once again, he motioned for her to come down. This time, she nodded to him and walked away from the window. He waited and watched the streets until she nervously stepped out the door. She was dressed for riding, like he had hoped. She wore a thick fur-lined cape over a cream-colored tunic and dark blue riding skirt. A grin broke over his face.

"What are you doing here?" she whispered.

His heart raced as he thought about the quickest way out of town.

"I have no time to explain right now, all I can say is you are in danger here. You must leave with me now before it is too late." He spoke honestly, knowing that every minute wasted talking was another chance for them to catch on.

Her eyebrows crumpled, obviously not understanding.

"I can't go, I have to wait here." Her voice was rising.

She understood something was terribly wrong, but was rightly confused by the way he had approached her. He had been worried about this. He knew she would be loyal to the Guardian in some way. That could not stop him right now. She had no idea what was coming out of the night to find her. Trust grabbed her arm and began pulling her with him.

"You have to believe me! I have horses waiting outside the walls. There are people here that want to hurt you." He pulled harder, nearly dragging her now.

"Then we should wait for the Guardian," she almost yelled, fighting his grasp.

He stopped then and gazed into her eyes. He would not leave her here. "Please believe me, Starlyn. It is not safe for you here. He will understand in time. You'll see, but for now your safety is the most important thing."

Her grey eyes were beginning to well up with water. She quickly wiped her face, then nodded. She had a strong will, that was for sure. He grabbed her arm again and pulled her down the street, hoping they had enough time to get away. They had gotten no more than two blocks from the inn before he heard a howl in the distance, closely followed by a second and even closer one. He resisted the urge to curse and began to run. Starlyn followed behind him obediently. When he glanced back, her face had gone ashen. She finally understood the danger.

He pulled her along as fast as he could, checking down side streets and alleys as they went. As if it would help. With the fog getting denser, he would be lucky to see ten feet in front of them. They rounded a corner and he slid to a stop, Starlyn bumping into his back with a gasp. This time, he did curse at his luck.

Selene stood in the middle of the street before them and he could almost feel the anger emanating from her. She wore the same red dress as before and her hair flowed loosely about her. The lamp light from nearby buildings made her brilliant blue eyes shine in the fog. Starlyn glanced at the woman then to Trust, brows knitted in confusion.

He looked for a way out, mentally going over the ways he could kill the woman before she had a chance to change. Then he caught a glimpse of a second glow of eyes behind them and knew that it was over. He turned back to Selene. They had run as far as they could go. His great plan to save the girl only led her into the hands of his enemies faster. Starlyn hugged close to him as

Selene walked down the street and stopped a few feet away. Her eyes burned into him.

"Where are you going, Trust? I thought you would introduce me to your friend," she said in her usual seductive way. She flashed him a toothy smile, showing her oversized canines to him.

To his amazement, Starlyn did not seem shocked by any of this. Maybe that was it, though. Maybe she truly was in shock. Selene's reflective eyes would normally send any commoner running and screaming bloody murder. Suddenly, a man from behind grabbed him with a steel grip and covered his mouth. How had the man snuck up so quickly? He was damn silent as he did it too. Trust fought in vain to get away, but found he was no match for the muscle of the man. Selene eyed him sadly, as if she was wasting something.

"Make sure he cannot use his hands or speak. He is beyond dangerous, and Gibbous will not tolerate a mistake," she hissed before turning to Starlyn, who stood there with wide eyes, not knowing what to do.

Her mouth opened slightly as if she was going to say something, but then she closed it again. He hoped that she would understand this was not his intention. The big man began to drag him into an alley, and this time Trust did not fight him. He got one more glimpse of Selene with her arm around Starlyn before he was engulfed by the darkness.

His anger flared; this was too much. The wolves had gone too far. Selene was right to know that he was dangerous. She had no idea exactly how dangerous he could be. He was a little insulted that they had only assigned one man to kill him. With the image of Starlyn disappearing into the mist with Selene burned into his mind, he knew it was time to show these dogs a thing or two about respect.

He relaxed his mind and focused on another world: his

home away from home. One thing the Night Runners were not aware of was he did not need any special symbols or incantations to travel. It was extremely painful for him, but he was able to leave his body by sheer will of mind. This made him even more dangerous than the wolves ever could have guessed.

His eyes rolled into the back of his head as he transitioned, and he was quick to latch on to the first demon that came near him in the underworld. He could feel the sweat roll down his face as he pulled the thing back with him. It screamed in a painful voice that only he could hear as he ripped into the world of the living.

By now, even if the man carrying him noticed that something was wrong, it was far too late. Trust opened his eyes and watched the shadow that followed them. The monster he had found was huge. It was hunched over in a sickening way and limped on a broken leg. It cracked sideways every time the beast put pressure on it.

Oh, how he loved it as soon as he laid eyes on it. It was fluid, unpredictable, and very dangerous. Trust watched its red eyes focus on him hungrily. The creature had no way of knowing Trust could take control of him now. How could it when it was surrounded by a world of tempting flesh? *Soon,* Trust thought to himself. *So very soon you will get your fill of blood.*

The man who held him was joined by a second, who held a knife in his hand. He did not hear if they exchanged words, only watched as the knife was raised to his neck for the killing blow. He focused his mind on the dark shadow nearby and let his body go limp in the arms of the man.

Once inside the demon's mind, he found the creature's senses were so different from a human's. Seeing through its eyes, everything thing seemed clearer. He could see the breath of the two men as they laughed at his unconscious body. He could see the lamplight sparkling off the fog in the distance. Most of all, he could see the blood of the men flowing underneath their fragile skins, and it excited his new senses beyond anything he had experienced before. This demon must be half starved.

Now, Trust did not fail to see the humor in any situation and this was no exception. He grinned broadly, showing his razor-sharp fangs. Usually, it was the demons that possessed men, but tonight it was Trust that possessed the demon. Ironic as it may be, it was another useful trick he had learned while growing up in another world.

He could feel the thick muscles of the malformed monster flex as he readied to pounce. He only had seconds before he would have no body to return to. With brutal power, he surged from the shadows. The demon's clawed hands met flesh and easily ripped the man with the knife in two. Blood sprayed everything, but he did not flinch. No, he did not slow at all. The demon's emotions were soaring, and it made his own mind rejoice at the sight of the blood.

The other man dropped Trust's human body in shock, but before he could scream, the demon grabbed both sides of his head and pulled it off his body.

He wailed with happiness. The demon's emotions were intoxicating. Trust fought the urge to find more victims. That was something he could not tolerate on his conscience.

He must act quickly to banish the demon back to the Underworld—once he let go of his grip, the creature would tear apart any living thing in sight.

When his eyes opened in his own body, he reached into his pocket and pulled out the bit of black quartz he had ready. The beast before him was already trying to retreat, yet Trust was faster. He tossed the stone at the monster, and it screamed in rage as the red light of the stone took it back to the Underworld.

He then found himself covered from head to toe in the

blood of the two men. It was a shame he had to ruin such fine clothes, but it could not be avoided. Demons were messy creatures. He did not bother to give the men a second glance as he ran back to the street where Selene had taken the girl. He had a score to settle with the woman, but for now he would be satisfied with getting Starlyn to safety. He just hoped Selene would be arrogant enough to try and fight him.

# Chapter Twenty-Six

The dream was like so many Starlyn had experienced in the past, yet at the same time different. She was in her field of clovers, but it was too hard to focus on them.

The voices were loud today, louder than any time before. She could tell that they were angry by the way they spoke. She tried to shut them out, but failed over and over again. She even tried to yell at them, but they ignored her. Finally, she found herself listening to them and trying to decipher what they were speaking about. Maybe even figure out why they were so mad.

"She is not ready yet! She does not even know how to control her sight." The female voice was softer than the others, but that did not stop her from sounding stern.

"We cannot interfere! That is the law we all agreed upon so long ago. The Dawn Child will either understand it or not. The decision is not ours; she must learn herself." She could not figure out if this voice was male or female.

"She will fail us all if we do not teach her!" a man's voice boomed, easily drowning out the other two.

A woman with a deep velvety voice spoke up. "Have faith in the child, she is stronger than we all know." The others began to mumble to themselves. "The Dawn Child is not alone in this. She has allies in the mortal world that can teach her as well as us." Starlyn heard some muffled agreements.

The soft-spoken women spoke again. "I have always said that it was too much to put on one mortal. She has been set up to fail."

Again, there were muffled agreements. Another voice began to speak, one that Starlyn vaguely recognized.

"It is not up to us to decide her course of action. It is true that her choices will affect the world she lives in dramatically, but you all must remember that we have given her the tools she needs. Do not rule out the people she has surrounded herself with. They are the keys to her freedom."

All the other voices stopped talking now. No more arguments came from any of them.

Starlyn was alone again in the field of clovers and found herself trying to figure out what it all meant. The Dawn Child was someone important, that was for sure. She also knew she had something to do with Trust, but that only made it more confusing. She could feel that the answers were right in front of her, but it was like they were in a different language that she could not understand.

Had the voices meant for her to hear at all? Was she supposed to know things she did not? Maybe she was one of the teachers they spoke about. That could explain why she was going to see the Elders. It was all so puzzling. She couldn't shake the feeling that there was something she was missing. Her frustration built the more she thought about it. Her temper was getting the better of her, and she shrieked at her own uselessness.

"Why don't you just leave me alone? I am sick of you being in my head!" she yelled at the top of her lungs, hoping the voices would hear.

That did not stop her from being startled when the voice she had recognized earlier responded.

"Have faith, child. *De Beschermer* will need your strength, and the Necromancer will need your guidance. If you have faith, you will be strong."

Starlyn stood amongst the clovers, stunned. She had absolutely no idea what the man was talking about.

"I don't understand. Have faith in what?" She waited a long time for the voice to return, but it did not.

Alone again, she pondered what the voice had said. The Guardian would need her strength? She found that hard to believe—he was the strongest person she had ever met. The Necromancer would need her guidance? That was absurd. Trust was helping her find her way. Maybe she was talking about a different Guardian and Necromancer.

As she pondered these things, she began to notice a familiar tune in the distance. She recognized it immediately as the song she had been humming lately. As soon as the comprehension hit her, she woke up. Her eyes popped open and she raised her head from the bed. When she glanced around the room, she noticed Jack-obee and Jack-obide were fast asleep by the door. Looking to the window, she realized it was dark out. How long had she been asleep? Sitting up, she rubbed her dry eyes, trying to remember why she had woken up. The Guardian was not here—that was certainly different. She had spent the past week with him always nearby, if not next to her, and she found it hard to admit that she was disappointed he was not here now.

The soft melody drifted through the room again, reminding her why she had woken up. It seemed to be coming from outside, so she got up and followed the sound to the window. When she glanced out into the streets, the outline of a man became visible in the shadows. The man was playing a flute until he gazed up and saw her. He put the flute away and waved at her as if he wanted her to come down. She hesitated, not sure if he meant for her to see or not, until he stepped further into the light. She smiled to herself; it was Trust. Then again, she should have realized that earlier when she'd heard the song. She glanced behind her at the twins. The Guardian would not like this at all. He waved at her again and she decided she better get rid of him before the Guardian came back. He was putting himself in danger by being here. She shivered, remembering the incident between the two at Cat's Cradle.

She quickly put her new boots on and was more than pleased to find that her toes could wiggle in them. Then she found the fur-lined cape the Guardian had ordered for her and left the room. It took all her effort not to breathe as she passed the brothers. She had thought the twins might wake when she left. Maybe they were heavy sleepers. She sped down the stairs and past the empty common room. Her heart raced the whole way, and she hoped she would not get caught by the Guardian.

When she left the building, she found Trust right where she had seen him last. His dark eyebrows were furrowed with worry that matched the stormy look in his dark brown eyes. She knew that something was wrong immediately.

"What are you doing here?" she whispered, almost afraid to hear the answer.

"I have no time to explain right now, all I can say is you are in danger here. You must leave with me now before it is too late." He spoke with urgency.

She had not expected this at all. Why would she leave with him if she had the Guardian to protect her? Where had he gone to, anyways?

"I can't go, I have to wait here." She could not control the panic that showed in her voice.

She would not leave without knowing he was okay. Trust's face hardened at her response. Clearly, he had expected her to leave. He suddenly reached over and grabbed her arm. She tried to break free, but his grip was firm.

"You have to believe me! I have horses waiting outside the walls. There are people here that want to hurt you."

She was in a near panic now. She had to stop him. The Guardian would want her to wait. She tried to plant her feet, but he pulled harder.

"Then we should wait for the Guardian." Her anger was rising with every step.

"Please believe me, Starlyn. It is not safe for you here. He will understand in time. You'll see, but for now your safety is the most important thing."

She fought the tears that were on the verge of falling. She knew she could trust him, but the thought of betraying the Guardian was unbearable. She met his eyes and saw that he was here to help her. She did not realize that she had nodded in agreement until he was pulling her down the road again.

She peered back at the inn, hoping that maybe she would see the Guardian there, but the streets were empty. He led her into the dark and she let him, not wanting to admit she was willing to go. She knew she should be worried about the danger he was talking about, but found that she could not focus on anything right now. All of this had happened so fast. As if the dream had not confused her enough, now she had to deal with Trust trying to save her from some unknown threat.

Suddenly, her thoughts were broken by a long howl in the distance. Before she could react, a second howl responded, much closer to where they were. Her heart dropped as it dawned on her exactly what the danger was. She remembered the fear of being alone in the dark. She remembered the hungry wolves surrounding her. This was no dream, though—this was real. The wolves had found her at last, and Trust was trying to stop them again.

He flinched at the sound of the howls, and then started to run. She followed without question. It all seemed like the right choice now. She understood everything he was trying to tell her earlier. They ran through the growing fog and past unmarked buildings. Her heart raced in time with her footsteps as they rounded the corner. She could see the outer wall now, and a surge of hope filled her. They would make it.

Trust suddenly stopped in front of her, making her bump into him. She peered around him cautiously. A woman stood by herself in the middle of the road. Why would he stop for that? She was surprisingly good looking, but that wouldn't stop Trust, would it? Then again, the woman was more than just pretty. She was the most beautiful thing Starlyn had ever seen. Her thin red dress draped over her lean figure astonishingly. Her hair, black as the night sky, hung below her knees, and her eyes were a brilliant blue. She sucked in her breath when she realized they reflected the lamplight the same way the Guardian's had. What did that mean?

She hugged closer to Trust, felt his body tense. The woman in front of them began to approach. Her stride was confident and so fluid that it could make any man crumble at her feet. She stopped a little way away and spoke in a voice that was as smooth as her walk.

"Where are you going, Trust? I thought you would introduce me to your friend." She smiled as she spoke, revealing an impressive row of sharp teeth.

She was one of the wolves. The realization clicked in Starlyn's head so loudly she thought the woman would have heard. This was a Night Runner in front of her, and she knew Trust by name. Why was the woman interested in *her*, though? Starlyn tried her best to keep her composure while the woman eyed her in a way that made her feel very insignificant.

Without any warning, Trust was ripped from her side. She turned and realized they were not alone with the woman. A very large man with golden brown eyes had Trust in his grasp with his big hand over Trust's mouth. Trust jerked against the man's hold with no success. She opened her mouth to protest, but the woman beat her to it.

"Make sure he cannot use his hands or speak. He is beyond dangerous, and Gibbous will not tolerate a mistake tonight." She said it as a threat and the man nodded in agreement before pulling Trust into the dark alleyway.

Trust's eyes shone with sympathy. It shocked her to see even now when he was in danger, he was still worried about her. The woman put her arm around Starlyn's shoulder and began to lead her away. She panicked and glanced back one last time toward the man that had tried to save her. In the last moments that Trust was visible, his face changed into something that could only be described as pure hate.

"Now, my sweet girl, I have an offer for you," the woman continued, as if nothing had happened and she had known Starlyn for years.

Instantly, Starlyn was on guard. Her gut told her this woman was dangerous. Everything about her seemed threatening, even though she had done nothing to threaten her directly. She decided quickly that if she were to put her will against the woman's, it would be her last mistake.

"But first I think introductions would be appropriate. I am Selene, and you are Starlyn DeTousan, am I correct?" She continued without waiting for an answer, somehow already knowing she was right. "I represent a very powerful person who wishes to meet you, Starlyn. This is the kind of invitation that only comes once in a lifetime. So may I suggest that you consider carefully. At the same time, I want you to remember that my time here is limited, so you must decide quickly."

How could she really expect Starlyn to even think about any kind of offer after watching Trust being dragged away? Her mother had always said that fear was a powerful tool, and Starlyn had never understood why someone would use it that way. Now she understood exactly what she meant. The scene with Trust was meant to scare her into agreeing. The only problem was she honestly did not believe that it was up to her. She would go if she agreed to or not.

"Do I really have a choice?" Starlyn responded numbly.

Right now, she was more worried about if her friends were still alive. Were they going to hurt Trust for helping her? Where was the Guardian? She couldn't help thinking yet again that none of this seemed real. She was so lost in her thoughts that she barely heard Selene laugh at her answer.

"Did you have a choice to see the Elders? I guarantee this offer will be much more profitable for you." Starlyn had never really thought about it like that before.

Had she really agreed to travel with the Guardian? She could not remember.

"How is it more ... profitable?" she asked bluntly, coming to her senses.

There was always a catch. She had a deep feeling that it was going to be a bad one, and she'd always had good instincts. She had learned to rely on them in tough situations, but this was by far the most pressure she had ever been under. Should she fight like Trust or should she go along with this charade?

"The Elders wish to use you, Starlyn. They wish to use you for their own personal gain. Honestly, they do not care what happens to you. They are selfish men that allow atrocious things to happen around them as long as they get what they want. You are truly an insignificant little girl to them. It is your talents they're after." She said this with such confidence that Starlyn almost believed her, but her pride would not let her.

"The Guardian would not allow it," she responded, trying to match Selene's secure tone.

"He is an instrument and nothing more. Do not forget that

he is a faithful servant to the Elders. He has protected you only because they have ordered it. What happens when you are all alone atop that mountain and they tell him to turn his back? Do you really believe that he would disobey ... for *you*?"

Starlyn had never really thought it through that much.

Of course he would do as he was ordered. If she had always known that, why did it hurt her pride so much to hear it out loud? She bit her lower lip in a hopeless effort to hide her worry.

"My mistress wishes to give you the tools you need in order to control your gifts," the woman continued.

Now Starlyn was really confused. Why would the Elders need to use her and what sort of talents was she supposed to have? This night was becoming more and more strange. Would her life ever make sense again?

"I think you have the wrong person," she told the woman, exasperated.

To her, it was obvious. Someone somewhere had made a very big mistake and now she was paying for it. How could they all think she was something other than what she obviously was? She was a sheepherder and nothing more. Selene was about to speak, but suddenly jerked her head toward the street to their left and growled deep in her throat. Shocked by her sudden change in mood, she followed Selene's line of sight and she felt her cheeks turn red.

She could barely see the man that walked through the fog toward them, but she did not need to see him to know who he was. She recognized the man dressed in black instantly by the way he moved. As hard as she fought it, a smile broke through her lips at the sight.

The Guardian was all right. She knew she was safe finally.

Selene had different thoughts, though. With a snarl, she

pushed Starlyn behind her as if she could hide the fact that she was there. The Guardian said nothing, just continued to walk toward them, the mist swirling around his feet as he moved.

Selene laughed unexpectedly in a musical way. "Stone Wolf, I was wondering when I would finally meet you."

Her confidence seemed uncalled for. Did she not realize how dangerous he was? The Guardian stopped at her words. The little light the lamps gave off lit up his green eyes. It took a moment before Starlyn realized Selene had called him something different. She tried hard to concentrate on what it was. Stone Wolf, she remembered suddenly. What in the hells did that mean?

"Are you surprised that I know your name? Can you not recognize mine?" Selene continued in her brazen way.

He started walking again without responding to her question.

"They could never beat that name out of you, could they —the humans, that is. Oh, but they tried to, didn't they?" Her voice turned into a velvet coo, causing him to stop again. "Do you know why that is? How very interesting, you really don't. Whatever are those humans teaching you?" She laughed softly.

"Let me enlighten you, then. Every Night Runner is born with their name. There is nothing that can change that. It is your birthright, your identity. But I see you have tried very hard to change. You will never be rid of your blood, Stone Wolf. It is time you quit trying."

Starlyn struggled to process everything she said. The eyes —that was why they had the same eyes. Why they both moved with the same abnormal grace. Her mind said it was impossible, but the proof had always been in front of her.

He was one of them. A Night Runner. No, not one of them, only one of their kind; she would never believe he would kill an innocent person. But when she looked at Selene, she could not say the same. The Guardian—or Stone Wolf?—was a Night Runner, that was for sure, but he was not the same as the woman before her.

Before she could pursue her thoughts any more, Stone Wolf unfastened his cape and let it drop to the ground. He was an intimidating man to gaze upon, even at a distance. He reached behind him and pulled out the sword that she had only seen used once.

Even though she was expecting the cold this time, it still took her breath away as it hit and she squeezed her eyes shut against the blast.

She opened her eyes and tried to focus in the suddenly bright blue street. The sword shone brighter than the sun and it burned to look at. Had it been like that before? The fog that had once surrounded all of them was no longer there. It floated down from the sky in the form of tiny ice crystals that glistened blue from the sword.

Selene growled louder this time and squatted down like she was ready to pounce. Stone Wolf continued to walk toward them. She had thought he was intimidating before—now he was terrifying. His head snapped to the right suddenly, and Starlyn was not prepared in any way for what she saw. The creature resembled a wolf but was three times the size of a man. It howled as it leapt from the roof, and her heart stopped for a moment. How could the Guardian kill that?

He faced the attacker with a calm that was disturbing. With what seemed like as little effort as a flick of his wrist, the huge broad sword swung to meet the wolf. When the sword passed by, the creature fell to the ground, howling in pain as it grabbed for its face. She hadn't even seen it hit the animal. When it moved its hands for a second, Starlyn could see the deep slash across its eyes that was covered in frost. She wondered just how sharp the weapon was. As the wolf rolled in blind pain, Stone Wolf stepped toward it and drove the sword easily into its back. The monster twitched once before its body was fully covered with frost.

Stone Wolf then turned smoothly and continued toward where Selene stood. Without realizing it, Starlyn had been slowly moving away from her. Standing with the woman was not the safest place to be right now. She was keeping her slow pace, backing away and hoping that Selene would not notice, when she caught a glimpse of movement out of the corner of her eye. Another wolf was approaching fast from a nearby alley. This one was grey in color and not as large as the first.

She hoped Stone Wolf had seen it too. He removed the throwing knives at his arm, then in the same fluid motion, he threw them toward the oncoming wolf. At the last minute, the beast raised its arm and the knives embedded into its forearm. If it had not reacted so quickly, they would have hit it square in the face. The Night Runner roared as it brushed the knives from its body. Stone Wolf faced the giant as it charged full speed toward him. He side-stepped the animal at the last possible moment, making Starlyn nearly yell out. The heavy sword arched through the air and decapitated the Night Runner with ease. The now frozen body slid to a stop a short distance away.

Selene's face turned white as she frantically searched for a way to escape. It was then she noticed how far Starlyn had gotten away from her.

She hunched over suddenly. With a howl that made Starlyn's ears hurt, her skin split down her back, revealing black fur. The sound of breaking bones was chilling as Selene contorted, her body taking on a new shape in front of her.

She stood and shook the remaining pieces of skin from her body. It was unbelievable to see the giant black wolf standing in the same place that the beautiful woman had. But the piercing blue eyes that looked out from the animal could not be mistaken for anyone else. Starlyn stumbled and fell back as Selene crouched, preparing to strike at her. She was overcome by the same terror she had felt so long ago in her dreams, but this time it was real. The wolves that were after her were real.

A deep bellow from the direction of Stone Wolf caught both of their attention just in time to see him drive the blue blade into the ground in front of him. They both watched as the ground around him frosted with ice. The circle began to grow at a rapid pace and it only took seconds for the frost to reach where they were.

"You will not touch her!" he snarled. With a jerk, he twisted the blade.

The ground erupted in front of him and continued to split all the way to where Selene crouched. She leapt over the torn-up ground toward Stone Wolf, who had already pulled his sword free. She ran straight toward him and then suddenly veered off to the right. With unnatural grace, she jumped to a nearby wall then pushed off and hit Stone Wolf in the chest hard, knocking him to the ground. Starlyn couldn't believe how fast it had all happened. Selene was on top of Stone Wolf with one of her massive paws pinning his sword arm. Watching in horror, Starlyn saw his blade had skidded out of reach.

She stood up, not worried that her fingers were numb from the cold ground, and ran a few steps toward them. She wasn't sure how she was going to help—she only knew that she could not sit and watch. She would not let him die for her.

As she neared, a hand shot out of nowhere and grabbed her arm. Her resulting scream caused Stone Wolf to look suddenly in her direction. The distraction only made things worse; Selene did not miss a beat and swiped one of her massive paws right at his head. He leaned away just in time, but her claws caught his mask, flinging it from his face.

Starlyn winced at her stupidity and watched the mask as it slid across the frosty ground. Her anger flared and she turned to fight off her captor. She swung her fist toward the attacker's face, only to stop herself halfway.

"Trust! You're alive!" Elation filled her soul.

She went to hug him but noticed he was covered from head to toe with blood. What had they done to him?

"Are you all right?" she stammered out.

"Did you really doubt me?" He smiled before bowing in his normal manner, then glanced over her shoulder and scowled. "I think it's time for the humans to leave."

Starlyn turned. The situation had changed. Selene was no longer pinning a man; where Stone Wolf had been lying there was a sandy colored wolf instead. This wolf was bigger than Selene and easily kicked her back into the nearest building. When she hit the wall, she also slammed into a lantern and shattered it, spattering the oil everywhere. The flames leapt up the wall, engulfing the building within seconds.

Trust grabbed Starlyn's arm again and tried pulling her away. She jerked free and stumbled to the ground, where she picked up the Guardian's mask, then turned and ran. She could hear howls in the distance, followed by screaming people, which only made her run faster.

They passed a group of men running toward where Trust and she had come from. Some of the men were yelling "fire!" and carrying buckets of water. Starlyn did not look back until she reached the outer wall.

At the sight of the trading post, her blood chilled. Half of the trading post was on fire. How had it spread so fast? Her thoughts turned dark as she remembered Stone Wolf was still in there somewhere, amongst the flames.

Trust gave her no time to think about going back. He pulled her through an open door that led into the stables. The horses were already waiting and he mounted his quickly. He turned when he realized she did not do the same. A familiar glossy black coat had caught her attention. The Guardian's stallion and her mare were also saddled and ready. She mounted her own mare and grabbed the reins of the stallion. She had expected the large animal to fight her, but it followed alongside her as she caught up with Trust. It was a shame that the pack animal was not with the other two. They could have used the supplies.

That did not matter right now. She was relieved beyond words to see that her friend Trust was still alive and with her. Even that good news was overshadowed by the fact that Stone Wolf was not. She could only hope that he was all right and would join them soon. It was the only thing she could do so she did not lose the battle with her emotions.

She already knew she had a lot of explaining to do once he saw Trust was with her. Glancing back, she saw *Vellei Bosje* was now completely engulfed in flames. They rose high above the town as villagers screamed. Was this all really because of her?

What a waste. All of these people were homeless now, all because someone had mistaken her for an important person. They rode as fast as the horses would go, straight into the *Bloed Hout*. As far as she could tell, the only thing that chased them was the mournful howls in the distance and her own guilty thoughts.

# Chapter Twenty-Seven

They rode for a long time—she could not say exactly how long—before they slowed. The horses were winded and a sweat covered their coats, except for Stone Wolf's stallion. He did not seem affected by the fast pace Trust had set for them. Starlyn's legs burned from the effort of staying on a horse as it ran. She had barely ridden a horse when she'd started her journey, let alone ran with one, and now it seemed like even her bones ached.

"Do you think Stone Wolf will find us?" she asked him after they finally slowed their pace.

He glanced back to her. "Who is Stone Wolf?"

"Stone Wolf is the name of my Guardian."

He nodded thoughtfully. "Yes, my dear, he will find us. Now, I think we should stop here for a while. I need to get cleaned up a bit. I fear that my clothes are unsalvageable. Besides, you look like you need a break too." He said it with a smile, but she could see the concern behind his eyes.

They stopped near the river *Aarde Bloed* and Trust went behind a few trees to change into something clean. Despite her soreness, she paced back and forth as she waited. Her adrenaline made her anxious. Stone Wolf should have caught up by now—at least she thought he should have.

Maybe he didn't know where she was. That would definitely be a problem. Did he even know she was okay? Had he seen her leave with Trust? The more she thought about it, the less likely it seemed. She had assumed he would simply meet up with them later and had never considered that he may not be able to. What if he was hurt and by himself? Her heart sped up again.

He would be mad at her, she was sure of it. Not only did she run away, but she was with the one man he had forbidden to be around her.

How was she going to explain why Trust was here? She would tell the truth. Maybe Stone Wolf would understand he was trying to protect her too. But then again, why would Trust be trying to help her? Stone Wolf had no idea that she had been seeing Trust in her dreams. Guilt washed through her. She should have told him. She should have told him everything as soon as it happened. Yet, why would she? It was none of his concern, after all. Furthermore, who she was with was none of his business either.

The quiet rustle of leaves made her forget what she was thinking about. She immediately stopped pacing, holding her breath as she listened. Nothing moved or made a sound, but she knew deep down that something was there.

"Trust?" She tried to sound normal but it came out as a whisper.

"No."

Her heart skipped a beat when she recognized Stone Wolf's voice.

She ran to where the voice came from and a smile broke across her face. When she got closer, she could see the outline of the familiar form in the dark and she threw her arms around him before she could think about it.

"I'm so glad you're all right," she burst out while hugging him as tight as she could.

He did not embrace her back, but he did not pull away either. Relief washed through her and the muscles in her neck relaxed. She finally let go and gazed into his green eyes, searching for some kind of reaction.

He wore a black scarf around his face, reminding her that she had his mask still. His eyes were hard and full of questions, but that did not stop her from smiling so much her cheeks hurt.

"Where is my mask?" he asked in a stern voice.

Her smile didn't falter. "I have it. I didn't want you to lose it."

She nearly skipped to where the horses were and pulled out the white mask. A thought occurred to her as she peered at the mask in her hands.

"Will you let me see your face?" she asked with her back to him.

She did not know why she had inquired, but once the idea was in her head, she knew that was what she wanted and she would not give it back until she saw the real him.

"No." He was so close to her his voice made her jump.

She turned around and he held out his hand, expecting her to give it up. She quickly hid it behind her back and smiled mischievously.

"I want to see your face." She knew she was pushing her luck here but did it anyways.

She stepped back a few paces so she was out of reach. His eyes narrowed.

"I do have the ability to take it from you," he whispered.

In her heart she knew it was true, but suddenly her pride reared up. She cocked her chin and stood straighter.

"You wouldn't." Now she was being reckless, but she wanted to put a face to the name.

He moved so quickly that she had no time to react. In the time it took for her to blink, he was on her, grabbing her arm. She instinctively pulled back, tripping on a nearby rock and pulling him down with her. They rolled down a small incline toward the river. All Starlyn could see was the black night flying by her and her only thought was that this was going to be very painful when it was all over. It took only a few seconds before she hit the flat ground hard, with Stone Wolf right behind her. She closed her eyes tight, waiting for the explosion of pain as her head snapped back toward the earth. After a breath, she realized it was over and no pain was coming.

Her eyes popped open to find Stone Wolf staring at her, his face only inches away. He had landed on top of her and somehow been able to cup her head with his hand before it struck the rock underneath. In the process of rolling down the hill, he had not only lost his cape but also the scarf around his face was gone.

All she could do was gape. He was much younger than she had expected, not even in his thirties yet. His face was angular in an appealing way and he had a strong jawline. The faintest trace of blond stubble was showing there. She took in his now familiar scent and sighed.

That was when she noticed his left cheek had three long gashes that ran all the way down his neck. They were red and puffy; they must be painful. She winced, realizing it had happened when Selene had knocked the mask from his face. It was Starlyn's fault that they were there.

She reached up without thinking, wanting to make it better for him. He flinched away.

"It will heal," he said as he reached over her head where his mask had landed.

Once he had it on again, he rolled off her. He pulled her up with him when he stood. She felt awkward suddenly. He had not wanted her to see his face, but she had forced him. It was a very selfish thing to do. In the end, he still chose to protect her instead of his identity.

"I'm sorry," she whispered.

They stared at each other for a while longer, neither of them knowing what to say. To her relief and horror, they were interrupted by Trust clearing his throat. Her eyes grew wide as she looked from Stone Wolf to Trust, then back again. When Stone Wolf let out a low growl, she stepped between them.

She panicked. "I can explain everything."

Stone Wolf stepped forward. Putting her hands on his chest, she pushed gently and he stopped.

"He was trying to help me. He just wanted to make sure I was safe." Her pleading did not seem to do any good. Stone Wolf's eyes blazed with anger.

"Starlyn, please, I can take it from here," Trust said boldly. "Guardian, I was on my way to see your Elders and staying in *Vellei Bosje* when I heard the commotion in town. Naturally, I went to investigate. The Night Runners were everywhere, so I decided to leave. That's when I noticed a familiar face running straight toward the fighting." He nodded in Starlyn's direction. "I could not let an innocent girl be hurt by foolishness, so I stopped her. She came with me willingly, might I add."

Starlyn nodded in agreement. It sounded like a reasonable explanation to her.

"Excuse me if I am skeptical," Stone Wolf responded. "Why, may I ask, were you going to *Hemel Deur*?"

Her heart sank. This was going to be more difficult to explain. Trust did not seem worried as he smiled at the Guardian.

"I am glad you did ask. I have had an open invitation to visit there for some time now. After running into the two of you at Cat's Cradle, I thought that I would use it. Which brings me to my next subject. I will travel with you the rest of the way." Trust's confidence was mesmerizing.

Her jaw dropped open, then Stone Wolf began to press against her hands again.

"I don't think so," he said between his teeth.

"I do. After all, it is very dangerous out here and I think an escort would be appropriate," Trust continued without missing a beat. "Contact your Elders and tell them Trust from the House of Riyaadh wishes to have an audience. Then you can see that I will indeed be accompanying you two."

She did not know what was going on and it was irritating to be left out of the conversation. She glared at Trust, letting him know that he should have brought her up to speed earlier, before she had to worry about them tearing into each other.

After a few moments of them staring at each other, Stone Wolf backed up from her and reached for his belt pouch. He pulled out a round blue stone about the size of an egg and rubbed it between his hands. She glanced to Trust to see if he was as confused as she was, but she was disappointed when he smiled confidently at her. That just made her more irritable.

The stone was now glowing from within. The more he rubbed it the brighter it got, until it lit the area around them. He tossed it to the ground a little way away from them and waited. The light continued to grow until it was bright enough to make her squint. In the middle of the light, she began to see the outline of a person. Rubbing her watery eyes, she had to make sure she was not imagining it. The shape began to solidify, and sure enough there was a slender man standing in the middle of the light. She took a step closer to Stone Wolf without realizing it. The slight man was pasty and pale with eyes that were black. He looked at Stone Wolf, then glanced at her. She thought he smiled but it came across more like a sneer.

"Guardian, I am glad to hear from you finally. Jack-obee and Jack-obide have already reported the incident at the trading post. I am filled with joy to see the both of you are safe. It is a shame about *Vellei Bosje*. We will send some funds to help repair it." His voice was high pitched and he seemed to overexaggerate some pronunciations.

"Trust from the House of Riyaadh wishes to accept his invitation," Stone Wolf said with such malice that Starlyn flinched slightly.

The man's smile faded. He stood there staring for a moment before turning. Trust bowed politely when the man noticed him.

"I have a proposition for the Elders that I believe they will be very interested in."

She frowned. What was he talking about? He hadn't told her any of this before, and she hated being left out. The man bowed in return, seemingly regaining his composure.

"As always, you are welcome in *Hemel Deur*, Trust from the House of Riyaadh." The man in the blue light flickered while he spoke. "I will inform the Elders that you wish an audience and send you a proper escort immediately."

Trust was shaking his head before the man finished. "I believe that I will travel with this very capable Guardian and the girl."

This man's eyes could not hide his contempt when he replied, "Another will be arranged, sir. This Guardian is for Starlyn and Starlyn alone."

Trust brought his hand up to stop the man. "I believe you do not understand. I *will* be traveling with Starlyn and her escort or I will not be coming at all."

Her head was beginning to hurt now and she gazed up

at Stone Wolf for some input, but he was unreadable. The man stood there for some time, thinking.

"Very well," the man said finally, then turned to the Guardian again. "You will escort Trust from the House of Riyaadh with Starlyn DeTousan, and I will receive your full report when you arrive." With that said, he vanished and the light went with him.

Starlyn found herself engulfed by the black of night. Her eyes were not used to the dark anymore. She felt Stone Wolf move by her and she reached out, grabbing hold of his arm. He bent his elbow and pulled her arm to hook his, then continued to the area where the stone was. She let him bend down to pick it up. When he straightened, she felt him turn again to where Trust had been standing.

"Before you travel anywhere with us, I need to know exactly what you are. I will not allow anything to hurt Starlyn." He spoke in a tone that made it sound final.

Her eyes burned from being awake so long, but she would not interrupt them.

"That seems only fair. Simply put, I am a Necromancer." Stone Wolf tensed at the word. "And I have encountered Starlyn in her dreams recently."

That caused Stone Wolf to take a step forward, and Starlyn pulled on his arm, reminding him to stay calm.

"I somehow pulled him into my dream. It was my fault," she admitted.

His eyes shone with betrayal and it hurt her heart to see his confidence in her falter.

"There it came to my attention that she has certain skills that I find very interesting," Trust continued, unaffected by the show of aggression.

"No matter how much you dislike it, you must realize that the girl is very gifted. Gifted in ways I have not seen before. My proposition is simple: I wish to help her learn to control her talents. I wish to teach her. I do not think that she could find anyone better than me to do that for her. Her talents seem to relate in many ways to my own." He paused, letting the words hang in the air. "Besides, I have heard your Elders have a very extensive library that I would love to see," he finished, as if they were having a casual conversation.

The news was just as new to her as it was to Stone Wolf. Could he really teach her? She didn't even think what she had done could be called talent. The more she thought about it, the more she liked the idea of being schooled by the man. Starlyn DeTousan, apprentice to the great necromancer Trust from the House of Riyaadh—she liked the sound of that. Her thoughts were suddenly broken when Stone Wolf spoke again.

"What is your relationship with the Night Runners? I can smell them all over you."

Trust did not miss a beat before responding. "I have information that may help your Elders in that area also, but that is for them, not you. As for the reason you smell them on me, well, that is because I killed two back in town."

Starlyn's mouth dropped open. She was impressed by his skill.

"Then there are only four or five left," Stone Wolf said. "Selene is still alive and Gibbous was not found. Silent Hunter, Faolan, Starless Night, and ..." He inhaled deeply. "Ulrica have been slain."

How on earth had he known all that? Trust, on the other hand, seemed immune to shock tonight.

"We cannot stay here," Stone Wolf continued. "If we ride through the night, we should reach *Bos Vlucht* by morning. It will be safe there."

The thought of riding more made Starlyn want to fall over and cry, but of course she knew Stone Wolf was right. He seemed to always be right in these situations.

Trust left them to make sure the horses were ready for travel. When Stone Wolf went to leave toward his horse, Starlyn grabbed his arm. He stopped but did not turn to her.

She stumbled over what to say to him, suddenly awkward. "I'm glad you are all right."

"You should have told me about him," he snapped. He turned toward her then, anger in his eyes. "I trusted you, but you went behind my back anyway."

Her heart hurt, immediately realizing the truth of his words. It had not occurred to her how her secret would affect their friendship.

"I'm sorry."

He walked to his horse without another word. He didn't assist her with her own steed but he waited, seething while she fumbled with the reigns.

The gravity of the night's events was beginning to weigh on her and it hurt to think she had lost her Guardian's trust. She looked to him, but he would not meet her eyes. He mounted his horse and set off, not looking back to see if they followed.

After the vision of the Guardian and the girl faded from sight, Iridium stood upon the stone dais, pondering the implications of the current turn of events. He was glad to hear that Trust from the House of Riyaadh was finally going to have an audience with the Elders. Iridium knew very well that the Necromancer was a powerful man. Furthermore, he knew how valuable he would be as an ally to the Elders. His current conundrum was more about the timing of it all.

The timing was impeccably fortunate to coincide with the arrival of the girl, but fortunate for whom? His main concern with the matter was why the Necromancer insisted on traveling with her. He said the girl's name in a familiar way, going as far as to use her first name. Trust's pedigree would normally not allow that. Even though he was notorious for being, among other things, a womanizer, he was always a gentleman.

Perhaps he was taken with the girl, then. Overall, that would not be a hindrance to the objectives he was given. In reality, it could be a benefit. If they succeeded in getting in good favor with the girl, perhaps then they would succeed at enlisting the use of the Necromancer's unique talents through her. Having a Necromancer with his abilities was a tantalizing idea, and Iridium could not help but be hopeful that the girl had indeed seduced the man. But then again, if she became a liability, then their bond would be not so ideal. He prayed it was the latter of the two.

Iridium smiled to himself, knowing success here would be an accomplishment worth rewarding and the Elders would be very generous. He wetted his lips at the thought. It did not overly bother him to be the eyes and ears of the Elders. The perks of the position were plentiful, but Iridium craved something more. He would not truly be great until he could make decisions on his own. That was something he kept well hidden in the back of his mind. If the Elders found his thoughts were so ambitious, he would be disposed of.

In the meantime, he would be satisfied with the influence he had on the Elders. His council was never taken lightly and for good reason. His council was always correct and in the best interest of the Elders. That was something Iridium made sure of. The news of the Necromancer would indeed be open to council and he could hardly contain his glee as he waited to hear what kind of proposition Trust had in mind. He casually walked down the corridor, but not too slowly, not wanting to keep the Elders waiting for this news. Normally he would not be away from his Elder for so long, but waiting for the Guardian's report was worth the time away. Besides, the Elder Coeus could reach him even if he was across the world.

Thinking of the Guardian reminded him of another thing that had irked him for many years. Stone Wolf, the Guardian assigned to escort the girl, had never failed to flaunt Iridium's lack of authority. He continually tested his patience and soon the Guardian of the Elite would have to be dealt with. It was a shame, really. Stone Wolf truly was an almost perfect example of the excellent training the Elders provided. It would have been so much more favorable to keep him around if only he would obey better.

Stone Wolf had always been strong headed, and Iridium was the one that argued to destroy him early on. The pup should have been killed with the rest of the pack, but the experiment went ahead anyway and now they had a full-grown Night Runner living among them. That was absurd in itself. Everyone knew Night Runners were unstable at best, but his trainers insisted that they had successfully taught him to control the animal side, and the Elders had allowed him to rise in rank, much to Iridium's disgust. It was only a matter of time before Stone Wolf would turn on them all.

Rounding the last corner, he walked into the largest room in the complex and nodded to the Keepers at the entrance. He paid no attention to the three Guardians lounging nearby and purposefully ignored the other two mages. Stepping up to the dais, he faced the inky blackness beyond. Standing as tall as his bony back would allow, he then bowed low to the mass of eternal night before him. The two mages took positions close behind him. Iridium smiled to himself, knowing they all wanted to know what he had discovered. Out of the corner of his eye, he saw the three Guardians stand straighter, paying attention now. He did not address the Elders until he was satisfied that all in the room were watching.

"My mighty gods, I have news from the Guardian Stone Wolf." He spoke dramatically, enjoying the way his voice echoed in the room. "The girl is safe, and they are now on their way to *Bos Vlucht* on schedule."

"You have already informed us of this news," the mage to the right interrupted.

Iridium shot him a glare. The darkness stayed silent, waiting.

"My great lords, please, I have more news," he said a bit too curtly. "The Necromancer known as Trust from the House of Riyaadh travels with them."

He waited for the news to set in.

"He wishes to make a proposition to you all and insisted on traveling with the girl."

Their silence began to make him uncomfortable. Was it possible he'd taken the news to be more important than it really was? No, only a month ago the Elders had mentioned their displeasure that the Necromancer had not yet come.

"You will show us all." The voice echoed from the darkness.

He recognized it as Elder Coeus. The mage had been prepared for this, and he opened his mind for the Elder to see. He felt the familiar inky black probe his thoughts just before the pain began.

That was the downfall of Coeus's talent. It was extremely painful. The blinding pain left as quickly as it had come, and Iridium realized he had fallen to the ground. He was covered in sweat and could not control the tremors that ran through his body.

He had barely regained his composure before he was assaulted again. He heard the voice directly in his mind. Coeus was pleased by the news and wanted to hear the Necromancer's proposition. The news of the girl's location was also very pleasing to them. She was closer than previously thought. She would be here shortly.

"Is everything ready for her arrival?" The question came from the shadows.

He knew the voice belonged to Elder Pontos. Iridium bowed again, certain that his credibility was still intact.

"All has been prepared, my lords. She will be treated like a queen." He smiled despite himself. A queen, indeed, as long as she provided what they wanted.

# Chapter Twenty-Eight

Trust rode with the pair in silence. It had been an awkward journey so far, and the tension between the two was palatable. It seemed a little too uncomfortable, considering their relationship was professional. Yet maybe he assumed incorrectly, maybe there was something more there.

No, that was impossible. The Guardian seemed to make it a point to ignore any questions Starlyn asked him. He rode with a straight back, keeping his distance from the girl.

Starlyn, on the other hand, could not stop herself from cycling between keeping her head down in obvious discomfort and glancing to the man to see if he was paying attention to her yet. Curious. They had not been together long, yet they seemed to have formed a friendship of some kind. A friendship he had torn apart in one night.

Guilt briefly washed through him. Maybe he could try to mend this himself? He pushed his horse forward so he rode between the two. Hoping to make his relationship with Starlyn clear, he decided to try to start a conversation.

"The girl is special, you know."

"It is not my place to know such things. She is my charge and nothing more."

The icy response shocked Trust mildly.

"She is a Dream Walker. Do you know how rare that is?"

Stone Wolf remained silent as they continued to ride. The man was beginning to irritate him. He was used to people listening when he spoke.

"A Dream Walker has the ability to manipulate their dreams. Some less talented people would call it lucid dreaming." He kept pace with the Guardian despite his obvious irritation. "Starlyn goes beyond lucid dreaming. I believe Starlyn can create dreams for herself, perhaps even affect the dreams of others."

He let the knowledge sink in some before continuing.

"Without the proper training, this could be disastrous not only for the girl, but for whoever's dream she enters as well. Despite what some believe, you can die in your dreams."

"Does that mean you can teach me to control someone else's dream too?" Starlyn chimed in.

He had momentarily forgotten the girl was with them.

"Not necessarily control their dream, but I believe you could influence it. Make them believe what you want them to see. Each person's abilities differ slightly from the next, but you have a good grasp on your own dreams already, so I think you would be adept in others as well."

She stared at him wide-eyed now. He could almost see the questions mulling about in her head.

"Is that why the Elders want to see me?" The question was directed at Stone Wolf.

He glanced briefly at her. "It is not my place to know the will of the gods."

Trust huffed at this. "Gods? They are not my gods."

The Guardian reined his stallion to a halt. His eyes bore into him. "If you do not respect *De Oudsten*, why do you travel to see them? Maybe you are an imposter, a threat I should be rid of."

The venom in his voice cut deep into Trust's pride. Maybe the man did not understand Trust was not ordinary either.

"Did you know who I was back at the Inn?"

The Guardian side-eyed him then. He could feel the hate radiate from him.

"Who you are means nothing to me."

"Be careful, my friend, I can ensure your afterlife is a very painful one," Trust stated through gritted teeth. He would not be talked down to.

"My soul will never see the Underworld; it is promised to another. Your threats are useless on me."

Trust ignored the cryptic words, too angry to register what he could mean. "Now listen to me, Guardian—"

"No, you will listen to me." Stone Wolf growled. "I am here to protect the girl. I will do as I am ordered and escort you to the Elders, but that does not mean you have to be conscious for me to do so."

He kicked his heels into his horse, forcing it to trot ahead of the two once more.

He peered to Starlyn, knowing she had heard the conversation, and found her eyes were still downcast. This was affecting her more than it should have. What exactly was their relationship?

The longer they kept moving, the more miserable Starlyn became. Her shoulders were tight with anxiety as the three of them continued in silence. She hated the tension between them, hated her sore thighs and back. Most of all, she hated herself for not being up front with Stone Wolf.

Guilt was heavy on her conscience as they continued toward the red woods. She wondered how long it would be before they arrived at their destination; how long before this horrible experience would be over?

Everything was beginning to wear on her already thin patience. Her stomach growled loudly, reminding her it had been hours since the last time she ate. Gods, what she would give for a meat pie right now.

"You know, not everyone has some poor soul back home eating for them."

She bit the inside of her cheek, knowing it was snappier than she meant it to be. Her frustration only grew when Stone Wolf appeared to ignore her yet again. He had done this since he had learned of Trust's involvement with her dreams and she was not amused.

"You can ignore me all you want, but *I* am stopping to eat!"

She pulled up hard on her horse's reins, causing it to neigh nervously. After the mare side-stepped a few feet, she finally regained control and dismounted. She did not bother to check and see if anyone followed suit. Her anger was beyond rational thought at this point.

She was too tired and too hungry to think about anything else. She had sat and stewed in her own guilt for hours. They were running on very little sleep, and she was beyond exhausted by now. She was over all of it.

She tore through her saddlebags, looking for something to eat. She found nothing in the first and sighed loudly, moving round to the second one. Here she found no source of nutrients, either. Seething now, she turned to see both men had dismounted and were tending to their own horses. They both made a point not to look at her.

"How long will you make me starve like this?" she snapped at last. "You have *both* been acting like spoiled children. Stop your damn bickering and get over it already! We are all stuck together now so we might as well figure out a way to be civil."

She took a deep breath and closed her eyes, willing herself to calm down. When she opened them again, Trust was holding out a small package wrapped in waxed paper. She gave him a withering smile as she snatched the package from his hands.

Inside she found hard bread and cheese. Her anger immediately began to fade. She took a grateful bite and excused herself quickly as she returned to tend to her own horse's needs. It was a foolish outburst she knew, but it did not change the fact they *were* acting immature. The whole time they had been together had been spent between tense silence and snappy passive aggressive comments.

The more she ate, the more her face became hot with embarrassment. Hadn't she been acting like a child as well? Hadn't she just thrown a fit because she was tired and hungry? It was all her fault; she should have been honest with Stone Wolf from the start. If she had, maybe they would still be friends right now. Maybe there wouldn't be this uncomfortable silence.

If she'd learned to control her Dream Walker powers sooner, maybe Trust wouldn't need to be traveling with them either. He was only coming because she needed his help. Her eyes began to well up.

It was her fault her father was alone doing the work of two right now. If she had been stronger perhaps, if she'd refused to go, then maybe none of this would have happened at all. The villagers would not have had their homes burned, those bandits would still be alive, Stone Wolf would have never met her.

The last thought hurt the most. Wetness trickled down her cheeks uncontrollably. She tried to stop the tears, but they just kept coming. Maybe she was not cut out to be an adventurer after all.

She most definitely was not a damsel being rescued by a knight; she was a child being kidnapped by a villain. No, that was backward. She was the villain here. If she wasn't in the picture, none of this would have happened.

Her heart ached with old emotions. Emotions she had hidden deep down for a very long time. The kind of emotions she had felt as a young girl who had no friends. The kind of emotions that made you feel like things might be better if you weren't around anymore.

Her trickle of tears now burst forth in waves. She dropped the food in her hand and openly sobbed into her horse's mane. Days of brutal riding, lack of sleep, and extreme adrenaline had finally caught up with her. She didn't care who saw, didn't care if her so-called friends judged her. Her heart ached and needed to release.

As she cried, she did not notice the man step behind her until he gently pulled on her shoulder to turn her. Stone Wolf stood in front of her, eyes full of worry. She tried to turn away but he wrapped her in his arms instead. She pressed her face deep into his shoulder and nearly wailed. She held on to him so tightly she thought she might break him.

She continued to cry as he put his hand to the back of her head and rested his head to hers. It was ugly but she didn't care. She sobbed until she couldn't breathe anymore, sobbed while snot ran down her chin. She clumsily wiped her face with her sleeve.

Stone Wolf picked her up and mounted his horse easily. He held her close and urged the great steed forward. She clung to him like a child but did not care. The smell of leather soothed her, and finally she began to ease. She hoped he would never let her go again.

# Chapter Twenty-Nine

Trust was shocked by what he had witnessed earlier. Not by Starlyn breaking down to tears. No, he was more so by her Guardian's reaction. He had never expected such a tender reaction from a minion of the Elders, especially since the same man had stated not so long ago he was there only to protect the girl. Their relationship turned out to be more and more complicated.

They had stopped some time ago and Starlyn had returned to her own horse. She now sleepily rode in silence. This silence did not carry the same tension as before. No, this silence was filled with exhaustion. They were all ready to be in a safe place where they could finally relax and process the events back in the traders' village.

Whenever he glanced at Starlyn he found her head lolled to one side, seemingly asleep. As he kept an eye on her, he watched the man in the mask out of the corner of his eye. The Guardian seemed tireless as he rode with perfect form, but that was not the reason he kept looking at him. It was the sword strapped to his back that kept catching his eye.

Trust found himself immensely attracted to the sword. Its mysteries called to him subtly even now. He could *feel* the damn thing pulsing as if it had its own heartbeat. If only he could get his hands on it for a while. He was sure he could figure out how its creator had constructed it.

He remembered his fear at seeing the blade itself, but the fear only made it more exciting. It had been a long time since anything seemed really dangerous to him.

He glanced back at Starlyn again and smiled to himself. It was always good to be reminded of what drove you in life. With all his skills and accomplishments, he was never satisfied. Then again, he did not think he would ever be content with staying still.

The night seemed endless but eventually he noticed the morning fighting its way through the dark. The black in the sky turned to dark blue, then eventually began to glow creamier. He found himself almost excited for the first time in many years.

He had never believed the Elders were a part of the old gods, so he never felt the need to accept their offer and stand before them. He did, however, believe the rumors regarding their library. It was full of ancient books, their topics ranging from science to legend. So much ancient knowledge in one place made his mouth water.

He hoped that something could be found about this Dawn Child and more importantly, the sword in possession of his current escort. Pelf's death was turning out to be a very good thing indeed.

Lost in his own musing, it took him a few moments before he noticed Starlyn had reined up on her mare. Both he and the Guardian did the same, and he wondered why she had stopped. Until this moment, he'd honestly thought she had mastered the art of sleeping in the saddle, but right now it was apparent that she was fully awake. She was gazing up to the trees with a very determined look on her face. He watched as shock registered on her face.

"There is someone in that tree." She spoke quietly.

Trust searched the tree. It seemed to be a normal tree to him. Then the wind drifted in and the leaves bobbed lightly. After a few moments, he noticed one area was not moving. To his surprise, his eyes focused on what was indeed a man. He blended into his surroundings so well Trust was shocked that she had seen him at all. He was more stunned when a throaty laugh came from Stone Wolf. Judging by Starlyn's expression, she was just as surprised as he was.

"Starlyn, you have a keen eye. I am sure that *Bewaarder* will not be happy that you spotted him." Stone Wolf was surprisingly upbeat.

The Guardian urged his stallion forward once again and Starlyn followed close behind, leaving Trust to follow the two.

"What is a *Bewaarder*?" she asked after she caught up to Stone Wolf.

"*Bewaarder* means Keeper," he explained. "That man is one of the keepers assigned to *Bos Vlucht* by *De Oudsten.* We are in a safe place now."

"I was always safe before," Starlyn said offhandedly.

They had obviously forgotten Trust was there at all. Normally that would bother him, but right now he found himself amused at the relationship the two of them had. When Starlyn finally glanced back, his suspicions were confirmed. Her smile disappeared and her face turned an amazing scarlet color. He grinned, knowing his smile would only make it worse for her.

As they continued on, Trust noticed buckets hanging on the trunks of the maples around them. Soon every tree had a bucket hanging on it, and he reminded himself there was a village in this area which worshipped the Elders and supported their beliefs by selling maple syrup.

Eventually a row of small huts came into view, each with a stream of smoke rising from its chimney. He counted twelve huts all together. They were all perfectly uniform and modest, if not sturdily constructed.

The huts gave way to a clearing that formed a kind of town square. Surrounding the clearing were five much larger buildings. The middle one was twice the size of the other four. In the center of the clearing was the largest tree Trust had ever laid eyes on. The canopy soared over the tops of the surrounding woods. Butterflies danced in the shafts of sunlight at the base of its massive trunk. The ground around the tree was bare of leaves and vegetation. The earth showed signs of wear from years of footfalls, permanently scarred.

Starlyn's gaze followed the trunk to the top, her head bent at an odd angle. Beyond the tree were more huts built in the same manner as the first ones they had passed. All of it seemed very neat and tidy. That seemed unusual to Trust; it was all too uniform in his eyes.

A few men and women dressed in common clothes milled about the clearing. All seemed to be busy doing some kind of errand, and smiles passed between them as they went about their business. That is, until they noticed the newcomers riding in. A few stopped to watch, while others hurried out of sight. It was apparent by their reactions that travelers were not seen here often.

Stone Wolf stopped near the largest building and dismounted. He tethered his stallion, and went to Starlyn's side and offered his hand in help. She clumsily tried to dismount herself and ended up falling into him instead. Trust could not help but smile when she shot him her best mean face. She righted herself with as much dignity as she could muster in her condition and looked as if she was about to stick her tongue out at him.

Trust chuckled lightly to himself and dismounted. She pushed him playfully and regained a little of her lost pride.

Glancing around the clearing, he found a man dressed in plain clothes striding across the clearing with a purposeful pace. He was closely followed by a man in a white mask and black cape, which marked him as a Guardian of the Elite. This

Guardian was not nearly as large as Stone Wolf, but his abilities were evident in the lethal grace with which he moved.

The newcomer gave him a thorough look, then went straight to Stone Wolf and clasped his arm in a familiar greeting.

"Stone Wolf, we have been waiting for you all morning," he said in a cheerful voice. "I'm glad to see you have made it without anything too major happening—besides, of course, the fire."

He winked at Starlyn before bowing low. "Starlyn DeTousan, it is an honor to finally meet you. My name is Pan and this is my Guardian, Orion. May I be the first to welcome you to *Bos Vlucht*." He said it proudly.

She beamed at him while turning red.

"I hope everything here will be to your liking." He turned to Trust. "Trust from the House of Riyaadh, we had word that you would also be our guest. The news was truly good to hear. I welcome you to *Bos Vlucht*." He bowed his head respectfully and Trust matched him with his own.

"Thank you for your hospitality," he replied politely, and Starlyn yawned out of the corner of his eye.

The Guardian Orion did not miss it either and waved a few women over that were watching from afar. He mumbled something to them that Trust did not hear. They nodded and all but one left.

"If you would please follow Dove, she will get some food for you while your accommodations are being readied." Orion motioned toward the girl who waited patiently.

Trust allowed Starlyn to go first, and she smiled gratefully before complying. Trust left Pan and the Guardians to trail behind.

They put their heads together and began to talk in hushed

tones. Trust tried his best to overhear their conversation but had no success. His attention was soon stolen by the appearance of a pair of seekers, twins to be exact. They approached with a confidence that came with any minion of the Elders, yet something else was there as well. It was the way they moved which seemed familiar somehow yet he could not exactly figure out what it was.

Starlyn waved at them sluggishly and they smiled brightly at the sight of her. Not until they both bowed to Stone Wolf did he realize who they were. These were the two in the room with Starlyn that he had put to sleep.

Stone Wolf gave them the slightest of nods and continued his conversation. The men fell into line with the rest of them as they followed the girl to their accommodations.

# Chapter Thirty

Starlyn stared blankly at her bowl of food. She lacked the strength to even lift the spoon. The conversations happening around her did not capture her interest anymore than the porridge in front of her did. She had never been so exhausted in her life. Each time she closed her eyes it seemed like an eternity before they opened again. She was fighting sleep, her eyes half shut when someone in the room laughed loudly. Her eyes flew open at the sound. Her mouth fell agape as she took in her surroundings.

She was not in the same room she had been seconds ago. Yes, it had the same furnishings and the same people were there, but somehow it had changed. It had become distorted or blurred around the edges, hazy even.

She blinked in an effort to clear her vision, but this only made it worse. Objects in the room were now discolored—not drastically, just not right. Each person in the room had changed as well. A soft blue-green glow seemed to radiate from their bodies. It was so subtle it took her a moment to understand what she was seeing. She could not explain why, but she knew the colors belonged there. Each person had their own subtle hue seemingly shining from within them. It was enthralling.

She watched each person while they shimmered with colors completely unique to each of them. Stone Wolf was the most startling of them all. He was haloed in so many different colors she couldn't keep track of them. Every color she could imagine surrounded him, almost as if his soul could not decide which color to be. It was so beautiful all she could do was watch as they moved in soft waves, going from warm to cold then warm again. She relaxed, becoming entranced by the sight. She smiled softly.

Stone Wolf stopped his conversation to watch her curious behavior. They stared at each other for what felt like an eternity. It was as if she could sense his emotions while she watched his colors move. Confusion, wariness, and something more subtle. Something warm she did not understand.

The rest of the room had fallen silent now, finally seeing the strange exchange between the two. She did not care—everything was right, everything was beautiful. *He* was beautiful, infinitely beautiful and full of so much emotion it made her dizzy trying to keep up.

What other wonders could she find? She stood, aware of the action but not in control of it. While she seemed to float toward the door, she thought she recognized a voice saying her name, maybe even asking a question, but paid no attention to it. There were much more important things to see.

Once outside, she was overcome by the splendor of the world. Every person had a color, each one different, yet they all produced a feeling of content within her. The trees, shrubs, and even the rocks on the ground were faintly outlined in their own soft colors.

She stood dumbfounded for a long time, taking everything in. Again, she heard voices and the mumbled noises seemed to refocus her a bit. It was then she saw the giant maple in the middle of the town. A warm yellow radiated wide around the tree, almost as if the sun itself stood there. She floated toward the tree, drawn by its warmth.

Her hand went to the trunk as soon as she was close

enough. The bark was coarse under her palm and warm to touch. Not warm from the midday sun—no, this was warm from within.

Needing to know more, she placed her other hand next to the first. There was a faint drumming within the tree itself. It seemed familiar, but she couldn't quite figure out why.

She concentrated on the rhythm, trying to remember what it was. With a jolt, she realized it was a heartbeat. Faint at first, but now she recognized it, she couldn't believe she had missed it before. Shocked, she snatched her hands away from the tree. How was this possible?

There was a faint rustle of leaves behind her and when she turned, she found Stone Wolf standing a few paces away. His brilliant green eyes were full of concern as he silently watched her. His aura was finally settling into a color that matched his enchanting eyes. She had so many questions for him.

"This tree is not a tree" was all she could think to say.

His reaction was only to nod once. How did he know?

She turned back to the tree and put her hands where she had placed them before. She felt the heartbeat right away and closed her eyes in order to sense it better. Something about the tree was wrong, like something was inside the tree, something she wanted to get out.

Focusing all her energy on the tree, she began to recognize the heartbeat had a source within the tree. She carefully wrapped her mind around the source. Cradling it softly, she pulled it toward her, much like she had with Trust during her nightmare. When it did not seem to move, she pulled with more strength. Slowly, the source of the beat was getting closer to the surface.

Sweat ran down her back. Her eyes pinched tighter as the effort became more strenuous. She was beginning to lose her grip on the source and her mind felt weak. She pushed herself further and with all the strength she had left, she gave one last hard pull.

The object did not move.

She swayed on her feet now. She had gone too far. The last thing she remembered was the feeling of falling, as the once colorful word around her went black.

# Chapter Thirty-One

Stone Wolf caught her before she could hit the ground. It was not until he'd made sure she was still breathing did Stone Wolf notice the commotion around him. Everyone rushed toward Pan, who had apparently passed out at the same time as Starlyn.

He watched Orion look toward him, then stand and reach for his sword. Stone Wolf's eyes narrowed, already forming a plan to get Starlyn to safety. His planning was interrupted by the growing crowd's gasps.

Pan had stood and the crowd around him went to their knees, bowing in respect. He was a powerful mage assigned to the Elders. Whatever Starlyn had done to the tree had affected him greatly.

"Please rise, all of you. Attend to the girl quickly, she may be the answer to our prayers," he said, placing a hand on Stone Wolf's shoulder.

He did not wait a second longer before standing, and easily hoisted Starlyn with him. The crowd that had gathered gave way and he ran to the house they had recently occupied.

He placed her on the bed delicately and his gut knotted. She was so pale. The door opened and closed behind him. He turned to find Trust staring with a face full of worry.

"What do you need of me?" Trust asked stoically.

He was not sure how to answer. All he could do was shake his head solemnly.

"Then I will do my best to find out what happened here. I have to be honest with you, I have been in contact with the girl for some time now. My skills may be of use. Her dreams are familiar to me; perhaps I can find her there now."

The thought of a Necromancer visiting Starlyn in her dreams made his blood turn cold. He stood straighter and met Trust's eyes, knowing it was the only option they had right now. No matter how much he did not like the idea, he had to do something, anything, to help Starlyn.

"Do it," he instructed before returning to the girl's side.

"The tree houses one of the Elders." A statement rather than a question.

Stone Wolf nodded in agreement, not paying attention to anything but Starlyn. He listened for Trust to leave the room before gently brushing a stray hair from her face.

"I will not lose you," he whispered into her ear.

Sometime later, Stone Wolf heard a soft knock on the door. Instinctively, he checked the sword at his side before calling out for the visitor to enter. Orion walked in with a determined stride, sweeping the room with cautious eyes. Stone Wolf stood straighter, until Pan followed close behind. He went to one knee.

"Stand up, my boy, please. I have had plenty of formality in my life; I do not wish it anymore."

Stone Wolf complied and briefly looked the man over. The mage was younger than most, newly assigned to the Elder after his other mage had died unexpectedly.

"How is she doing?"

"No change as of yet. She does not seem to be in pain."

Pan nodded to himself, still looking at Starlyn. "And how are you doing?" he asked bluntly.

Stone Wolf hesitated. "I will not fail to fulfill my mission. *De Oudsten* have entrusted me to bring her to *Hemel Dour* and I will."

The mage eyed him briefly before smiling. "I have heard many stories of your accomplishments. You have quite the reputation. The Guardian who is a Night Runner. The man who holds the honor of bearing the legendary sword *Niets*, not an easy task." Pan's gaze drifted to the sword on Stone Wolf's back. "I do not doubt your ability to accomplish your mission, but that is not what I asked you. How are you dealing with her being in this state?"

Once again Stone Wolf found himself confused at the meaning behind the Elder's words. Starlyn lay in bed, still pale beyond imagining. His heart sank knowing he could do nothing for her.

"I will accomplish the mission given to me." It was the only answer he knew how to give.

"The Necromancer said he is going to try to find her beyond the gates. He is a very remarkable man, that one. He also has a remarkable reputation. Why is it he travels with you?"

"He has told me that he wishes to take up a long-standing invitation from *De Oudsten*, though that is not his real reasoning. I have yet to discover his true intentions."

Pan nodded to himself before walking toward the door. "She is an important part of all our futures. I believe she can free the Elder from the tree. I believe she was very close to doing so when she fainted."

Stone Wolf chewed on this information for a time. Could she really be the one?

"Remember, not all have the same goals in mind. There are many who wish to see this girl fail to save the Elders. Be careful who you trust, Guardian."

# Chapter Thirty-Two

Trust wasted no time commandeering a house, and was able to secure the assistance of a Keeper to watch the door for him. He cleared out the furniture, leaving an open floor to work with. After carefully drawing the protective circle and ruins on the floor, he sat comfortably within the middle. Whatever had happened in the clearing was something he'd never seen before and that was well worth the investigation. His mind raced in so many directions. Were the rumors of the Elders true? Were they really gods and not a fanatic cult? The thought sent him reeling.

Closing his eyes, he leveled his breathing. He imagined the first gate with its misty walls and chilled air. He took a deep breath and could smell damp earth around him. The familiarity of the first gate always soothed him—he was home. When he opened his eyes, he knew instantly that he was not alone. He turned to find Selene in her human form, the wispy mist pooled at her feet. She was dressed in her usual blood-red gown, which draped over her body almost as fluidly as the mist around her. She stared at him with a look that burned into his soul.

"I have been waiting for you," she said with a velvety sneer. "You have not been very faithful, have you?" Her tone was darker than usual.

To say she was mad would have been a dire understatement.

"Your impudence will not be tolerated any longer. I assure you that I will enjoy making sure your soul never returns to the world of the living." Her smile made his gut turn.

He had not anticipated this. His mind raced as he watched her form shift fluidly to the wolf. Red folds of cloth mixed with black fur, leaving strange red markings across her body. His body tensed.

"I'm very sorry to disappoint you, my dear lady, but I do not intend to die today," he said confidently, a smile forming on his lips.

He flipped out his flute as she sprang toward him. With a quick flick of his wrist, the mist that floated around them solidified, suspending Selene in midair. He gave a small shake of his head, almost feeling sorry for her. Sometimes it made him sad to realize how easy it was for him to manipulate the fabric of the gates. Then again, he would not be alive right now if it was not that way.

"Did you really think it would be that easy? I suppose you did." He raised his flute to his lips and began a deep melody.

It was filled with melancholy, which always seemed fitting for its purpose. Selene's eyes widened with panic when she realized what was about to happen. The song was one of permanence, one that would cast her beyond the final gate, from which there was no way to return.

He was almost finished when the hair on his arms stood up straight. He cursed to himself before looking left into the face of the black form that was so near to him, much too close for comfort. The minions of the underworld were getting better at approaching him. The hooded figure reached out just as Trust turned to run. Selene laughed behind him as her bonds released.

"Damn," he thought out loud.

Starlyn had said that they were not allowed to harm him. Well, apparently she was mistaken. He raced ahead looking for a quick way out, but none were found. He skidded to a stop; two more dark forms were approaching on the horizon. He pulled his flute out again, swerving left just in time to dodge the cold hand of the creature that followed him. He attempted to lift the flute to his lips when he was tackled to the ground by Selene.

Pinned, he gazed into her ice blue eyes and a chill crawled down his spine. She knocked his flute out of reach and bared her teeth. Hot breath filled his face and the smell of rotting meat enveloped his senses. Quick as lightning, she lunged for his throat.

Time slowed and then stopped. Three hooded figures stood behind Selene. The middle figure reached out and lightly touched her shoulder. Her wolf form ripped open, then disappeared into the mist as if she had never been there.

The world began to move at normal speeds again and Trust sat up. Their faces were an abyss of black that never seemed to end. The display of power was phenomenal; he had not seen anything like it before. How in the hells had the creatures stopped *everything*? Not just holding something captive, they had actually stopped time. That was a trick he needed to learn. Furthermore, what had they done to Selene?

The middle figure, the one that had destroyed Selene, removed its hood. Trust could not hold back his smile at the sight of his old friend. The demon hissed softly and Trust recognized that he was laughing. Trust stood and readjusted himself, brushing off the non-existent dirt from his clothes, before returning his attention to the oozing humanoid in front of him.

"This is a most pleasant surprise, my friend. What do I owe the honor?" Trust bowed his head.

"The Night Runner did not have permission to be here. Belial does not look kindly upon uninvited guests," he bubbled in return.

Trust did not hide his confusion. "Since when did you

start to do the bidding of the underworld?" he asked skeptically.

"There are many things you do not know, old friend. There are many things you cannot know."

Trust simply nodded in agreement, though his curiosity wanted to push the subject. He knew it would be a lost cause. His friendship with the demon was complex and, most of all, forbidden. His knowledge of demonology was extensive thanks to the one standing before him, yet he knew almost nothing about the creature. So many unanswered questions irritated him.

Trust reminded himself Starlyn needed him. "Well, this unintentional rescue is very appreciated, though I am sure the ruler of this great underworld will be upset by it. Until next time, friend."

With a wave, Trust turned and retrieved his lost flute. When he turned back, he found the three demons were now gone. Shaking the odd occurrence from his mind, he refocused on why he was here: Starlyn.

He lifted the flute and played Starlyn's song. It did not take as long as he thought before getting a response. Following the trail of light, no larger than a thin rope, he soon found himself standing above the dream hole. He took a deep breath before stepping forward. He had no idea what to expect when he got inside.

He walked through the black void, which once again had no end. He had been to this dream before. It reminded him of the first time he had met Starlyn here. He almost expected to hear the wolves howling in the distance again. The sounds he heard were not wolves, though, they were voices. He looked around, trying to find their source. There was nothing here except blackness. No outlines of hills or a hint of stars. So, this was not like her first dream at all.

The voices were not speaking to him, though he could clearly hear what they were saying.

"Will the child recover?" a man asked.

"It is unclear at this time; she has yet to reform her mind after the shock of the awakening," a child's voice answered.

"So she is lost to us, then. It will be a shame to not see the contract fulfilled," a third voice chimed in.

"We are not alone." The man spoke suddenly, and the world around him went silent.

A cold tremor of fear formed in his gut. He had never experienced silence as he did now. The sound of his own breathing was absent, the void eating all noise around him.

"Starlyn!" Trust shouted, yet his voice was lost instantly.

The sensation did not help his nerves at all. He reached into his pouch and produced a short stick about the size of his thumb and made of white wood. He held it between his hands and carefully began to blow on it. When he opened his hands again, the stick shone bright white, which normally would have lit a small room with its light. To his disappointment, the light did not shine into this darkness around him. Dreams were always harder to manipulate than the gates, mainly because there was no specific set of rules here. Only the owner of the dream knew the rules of the world they created.

"Starlyn!" he yelled again, with the same outcome as before. "Damn, girl, where are you?"

He had one more idea that he hoped would get the girl's attention. If the voices he'd heard earlier were right, then the girl needed to find herself again.

Trust withdrew his flute. He'd had the instrument for so long now it seemed like a part of him. This was his last option to find the girl here. He prayed to gods he did not worship and held the flute to his lips. Starlyn's song began, as sweet as ever. She had such a playful, innocent soul and he loved playing her song. He played with all of his heart, calling out mentally to her soul. He did not know how much time had passed as he played, but it did not matter.

Eventually, he began to doubt his efforts; maybe the girl really was lost to them. Maybe he had finally found a challenge he could not manipulate or overcome. He was not sure which one worried him more. He stopped playing, feeling utterly alone and knowing he had failed to save her. His gut twisted at the realization she may actually be gone forever and there was nothing he could do.

Then he noticed a small white dot above him. It was like a lone star but different—it did not produce light like a star. Like a pin hole in a cloth, you could see the light through it. The object seemed to grow. He watched almost entranced as the whiteness slowly consumed the sky, then the surface he stood on. The blackness began to swirl in one spot in front of him. It was still disturbingly quiet and the changes around him produced no noise at all. The blackness disappeared, then reformed again closer to him. It moved fluidly like satin as it eventually took form.

Trust found himself standing in a stark white environment face to face with Starlyn. She wore the inky blackness as a dress. She was normally in white when she was dreaming. Why the change? Confusion shone within her soft grey eyes.

"Who are you?" Her words echoed for what seemed like forever before the world went silent again.

"You don't recognize me?" He spoke carefully, not fully understanding her condition. She seemed lost in thought for a long time. "Trust, my name is Trust," he said at last.

She paused for a moment before responding. "What are you doing here?" Her lack of emotion was disturbing. Her voice was the only sound that echoed in this place, making the hair on the back of his neck stand up.

"I am here to bring you home."

"I am home. You do not belong here." Her words had power behind them. He could feel his soul wanting to leave. He had to mentally fight the compulsion to leave immediately.

"Starlyn, you have to wake up. You have to come back to us." His efforts to fight her words weren't working.

"Leave," she said before turning her back to him.

"Stone Wolf needs you." As he hoped, she stopped and turned back toward him. Her eyes softened slightly. He could finally see some recognition behind them. "He waits for you. Right now, he stands by your bed hoping you will wake up."

Her eyes closed and a single tear fell down her face.

"Go!" she screamed.

The need to be gone consumed him. In the back of his mind he knew he should stay, but he couldn't fight the urge to run. So ran he did.

# Chapter Thirty-Three

Starlyn opened her eyes, or at least she tried to. Her eyelids were sticky and heavy, refusing to budge. Eventually, she managed to crack them open enough to be blinded by the light that shone through the window next to her. Her eyes were grainy but she succeeded in holding them open long enough to adjust to the light.

She took in the room around her. She was in a bed and covered up to the chin with a thick blanket. The room was vaguely familiar and she began to remember being here before. Her mind was dull, almost fuzzy, when she tried to concentrate.

She vaguely remembered the tree outside and the colors that had surrounded everything. She remembered pulling something out of that tree, but did not know what.

She tried to move her arms out from under the blankets, but could not muster the energy to do so. Everything ached, everything felt heavy. Why was she so tired?

Sitting next to the bed was Stone Wolf. He sat slightly slumped over, which was very uncharacteristic of him. He looked worried, she realized, actually worried. It was an unfamiliar emotion to see coming from the confident man she'd come to know. Why was he hurting? She just could not remember.

Suddenly, his head bolted up like he knew she was awake. When his eyes locked on to hers, she saw so many emotions that she could not keep up with them. Relief washed over her; she was always safe with him.

"You are awake." It was a statement more than a question. He reached for a cup of water and carefully gave her some. The cool water felt amazing going down her throat. She did not attempt to speak; she was much too tired. Her eyes finally gave up and closed once again.

The next time Starlyn opened her eyes, the room was different. It was dark, lit only by one candle, and Trust stood over, her chanting in a language she did not understand. Her eyes opened and he smiled brightly.

"Keep resting, girl, no need to hurry," he said softly before her eyes closed and she drifted off to sleep once again.

She did not know how much time had passed, but the third time she managed to open her eyes she felt completely refreshed. The strong aroma of something tasty filled the room, and her stomach groaned loudly in response. Her eyes locked on to a steaming bowl next to her bed, along with a half loaf of fresh bread. She pushed herself up into a sitting position and began to reach for the bowl. She was surprised when someone else's hand reached it first.

Stone Wolf picked up the bowl and handed it to her. She wasted no time before filling her mouth with the delicious stew. The meat was perfectly tender, accompanied by carrots, potatoes, and mushrooms. It was all excellently seasoned and tasted like heaven. It didn't take long before the bowl was empty. Then she began to consume the bread, using it to sop up whatever was left of the stew. When that too was completely gone, she sat back with her hands on her stuffed belly.

"Feeling better?" Stone Wolf asked.

"Very much so," she replied. "How long has it been?"

"Three days."

The words shocked her; it seemed like a day, maybe two at most. She moved the blankets and began to get up. Once on her feet, she wavered, not used to so much activity.

"Slow down, there's no need to hurry," Stone Wolf said as he grabbed her arm to help steady her.

"The sooner I get to *Hemel Deur* the sooner I get home. My parents have to be worried about me." The grand adventure did not seem so glamorous anymore.

She was tired of the world already. Now that she had experienced the strange events, all she wanted was to be home again.

"You still need to recover more. We are not leaving until you are fully rested." His tone said there would be no argument.

She sat back on the bed, realizing he was right. Moments later, Trust entered the room without knocking. His smile brightened her mood slightly.

"Starlyn, it is always a wonderful day when you are here." His upbeat attitude was contagious and she found herself grinning in response as Stone Wolf rolled his eyes.

"I see you ate," Trust said, looking at the empty bowl. "You should really try Dove's apple pie, it is heavenly." He winked.

"I am sure that is not the only thing you find heavenly about her, Necromancer," Stone Wolf said sarcastically.

Starlyn laughed at their banter. They were growing on each other—what had happened while she slept?

"The food was good and I can't wait to try the pie." She smiled.

"So tell me, my dear girl, do you remember what happened?" Trust did not miss a beat, his smile never wavering.

Starlyn sighed. "Not really, only parts," she said softly.

Trust nodded like he'd suspected that.

"Well, I have someone outside that may be able to help with that." He stood straighter, and then walked toward the door.

Stone Wolf placed himself in front of her in a protective way that had begun to feel familiar.

When Pan entered the room followed by Orion, Stone Wolf fell to one knee, still keeping her behind him.

"I'm getting sick of you always doing that, Guardian," Pan said with a chuckle, and Stone Wolf stood again. The mage looked her over and smiled warmly at her. "Can you walk? I have much to tell you, girl."

She looked to her friends before nodding in agreement.

She carefully put her feet on the floor and Trust slid over a pair of slippers, which she put on. She realized she wore nothing but a camisole when Trust handed her a furry robe. She smiled gratefully at him and let Pan lead her from the small hut.

The fall air felt great in her lungs as she breathed in the woody smells around her. She felt so much better already. The two Guardians followed closely behind them. Pan leaned in a bit closer and spoke in a hushed tone.

"I never believed them, you know. My Elders like to boast, yet I never believed that they had found you. Yet here you are, and I have seen you do what I thought was impossible. Do you know how special you are?" He smiled brightly at her.

"I don't know what I did."

His smile never faltered. "Where should I begin? To be blunt, I believe you have the power to save the Elders' souls."

Her jaw went slack.

"You see, it was a world much different when the Elders lived as men. There were thirteen brothers originally, but now only five survive."

He was silent for a moment, as if thinking about what to say next.

"They were cursed ages ago and their souls trapped within trees. This made them vulnerable and it did not take long for enemies to figure out this weakness. Many of my Elders fell before two summers had passed." He paused briefly to accept an apple from a passerby. He handed it to her.

"My clan of mages proposed a deal with the Elders and a pact was formed. Since then, each Elder has been assigned a consort. A living host waiting to receive the soul when the time is right."

She nodded with understanding. She had heard this legend before. Gods entombed in trees, cursed to live among mortals for eternity. Mystery surrounded them though, and she was afraid to hear more. All she knew was their followers were considered fanatics by most.

"I am the consort for the Elder in the maple tree, and I believe you have the ability to release his soul from the curse."

She stopped walking, trying to process what he was telling her.

"H-h-how?" she managed to choke out.

He chuckled. "I have no idea!"

It was a lot for her take in. She could free his soul? Is that what she'd pulled at inside of the tree? It was all so confusing. Did gods even have souls?

"I understand this is a lot to process, and I do not expect you to be able to accomplish this immediately. I know the Necromancer wishes to help you learn your skills. I hope you will stay with us for a time."

She began to feel weak again. Stone Wolf seemed to recognize this and was instantly at her side. Taking her arm, he met the mage's eyes boldly.

"She must return now."

The mage nodded in agreement. "We will speak more on this soon"

Stone wasted no time escorting her back to her room,

where he assisted her to lie down once again. She was still exhausted from the ordeal. He reached again for the cup of water and helped her take a small drink.

"Thank you."

"There is no need to overexert yourself. We are safe here."

Safe. It seemed like such a hard concept to grasp suddenly. Not long ago she wouldn't have used the word to describe any part of her life. Now, though, would she ever feel safe again?

# Chapter Thirty-Four

"Focus, girl."

Trust tried to get Starlyn to concentrate, but was finding teaching her was much like herding chickens.

"I'm trying! I don't understand how meda ... meda—"

"Meditation."

"Right! How's that going to help me?"

Trust sighed deeply. They had been sitting in the town center by the great maple tree for hours trying to get the girl into some sort of calm state. She fought him on every turn. This was only the first step to unlocking her potential and already she was having difficulties.

"If we can clear your mind, then we may be able to focus on your abilities better. You must have a clean slate to begin with." He did not miss when she rolled her eyes at him.

This teaching thing was becoming more of a pain than he originally anticipated, and he was beginning to regret his decision to help the girl.

"I just can't get rid of all the thoughts in my head."

"Well, let us try it a different way. Let's not try to be rid of the thoughts. Let us simply acknowledge they are there and not dwell on them."

Her jaw went slack in obvious confusion.

"Okay, so your mind is like the sky and clouds are like your thoughts. Some days there are more clouds, other days there is more blue sky. Your goal is to focus on the blue sky rather than being distracted by the clouds. Once you're able to do this, you can start moving inward and perhaps find the source of your abilities."

She nodded and he was surprised she did not argue this time. He watched her take a deep breath and close her eyes again.

"... blue sky ..." she whispered.

He smiled then, watching her sit cross legged amongst the other villagers underneath the great maple. Her stubbornness knew no bounds, but he still enjoyed his time with her. She had a quick sort of humor about her and he liked their conversations despite her argumentative ways.

Her brows began to furrow tight and he knew she was not focusing on the blue sky anymore.

"Acknowledge the clouds but let them float by."

She peeked one eye open and flopped back with a *humph* when he caught her looking.

"It's impossible. I'm not made to mediate."

"Meditate," he corrected.

"Whatever! There has to be a different way. This is wasting time."

She lay on her back for a long time, actually looking at the blue sky and clouds.

"Okay, well, maybe we can try a different approach. Come place your hand upon this sapling."

She was skeptical but finally complied, gently cupping the new growth leaves of the nearby maple tree sapling.

"Now think of your blue sky and ignore those clouds. Once you have it, think about the leaves you hold. Think deeper than the leaf, think about the veins in the leaf and life that drives it. Why does it grow to the sun, why does it wither without water?"

Starlyn was quiet for a long time.

"It grows in the sun … withers without water …" she whispered to herself. "It's alive … in my hand."

He watched her intently now. She was putting something together in her mind. He could feel it, she was getting close.

"It's alive in my hand." She was barely audible now. "Where does your life come from? How do I find it?"

She had finally reached the calm she needed—maybe not quite a meditative state, but close. He knew she could do this, knew with all his heart she was powerful enough to master her gifts.

Suddenly, the leaf she held twitched. No, he had to have imagined it. But then it twitched again, this time pulling away from her hand altogether. The leaf began to grow larger in front of his eyes. How was this possible? As suddenly as it had begun, the leaf wilted, drooping back to Starlyn's hand.

She let out a noisy breath and stared at the sad sapling. "I hurt it … I didn't mean to." Her voice cracked.

"My dear girl, do you know what you have done?"

She shook her head, dark circles forming under her eyes. The feat had taken a lot out of her. "Should I try again?"

He was impressed by her will.

"If you feel as though you can."

She nodded again and palmed the wilted leaf. She closed her eyes and her eyebrows furrowed together. A sheen of sweat began to form on her forehead as she tried to make the sapling move. He waited expectantly, but it soon became apparent nothing was happening.

"It's not the same now!" She hit the leaf away from her. "There's no life left in it, I can't make it move."

Fascinating.

"What does that mean?" he prompted. "Tell me before you

lose it."

"It was alive in my hand. I could feel its life. I pushed it to grow. I don't know what happened, it just went away so quickly. When I tried it again, there was no life there anymore."

No life anymore? This was reminding him very much of his necromancer skills. He was able to use death for his own purposes, but was it possible she was able to use life in the same way? The possibilities were mind blowing.

Starlyn sagged against the Elder Tree. He was impressed she was able to stay awake. He would not push her any further today, the poor girl had been through so much in the past few days.

"Tonight let us explore the Dream Walker side and see if we can find an answer there."

"So no more clouds today?"

He shook his head, and she smiled weakly.

She was not always the most cooperative student, but he had a feeling once she gained control she would become one of the most powerful people he had ever known.

# Chapter Thirty-Five

Training was awful. Trust pushed her day and night to try to find her triggers for her newfound abilities. It led her to be exhausted constantly, and it was frustrating how little progress she was making. Her Dream Walking was improving but still felt unpredictable. While awake, it was near impossible to feel life like she had inside the Elder Tree.

The moonlight outside of her window lit the night beautifully, its white glow highlighting the roofs of other houses. She rolled over in bed again, trying to force herself to sleep with no success.

The progress she had made with the sapling seemed to be a fluke at this point. She had not yet come close to replicating it. She was beyond frustrated and it was keeping her up at night. Now she found herself wide awake despite her eyes burning with exhaustion. She was tired of being the student, tired of everyone waiting for her to do the impossible. She wanted to go home.

Too restless to lay here any longer, she rose from bed. The room was empty and she hoped she'd be able to slip away unnoticed. It had been what felt like an eternity since she'd had any time to herself and the full moon outside was too tempting to let the opportunity pass her by.

Outside, she embraced the chill in the air with open arms. It was absolutely invigorating. The bright moon lit up the world around her, giving it a surreal feeling. She loved how peaceful it all was. The woods surrounding her seemed magical as she wandered the outskirts of the village, enjoying the loneliness of the trees.

It felt like fairy folk would appear from behind the trees and take her away with them. She laughed inwardly at that. She had been thinking of fairy tales when she'd seen Night Runners in person and felt gods trapped in trees. Maybe *she* was fairy folk.

She continued lazily walking past each tree and placing her hand upon the trunk. With each touch, there was no response, but she continued to brush her fingers against the rough bark of every tree. Maybe one would respond to her, maybe one would tell her what she needed to do next.

She wandered toward the center of the village, loving the emptiness of it all. She had grown up spending much of her time alone and she had been suffocated by attention lately. She was at home when she was by herself, finally able to slow down and reflect.

So much had happened in the time since she'd started this journey. She never dreamed she would be here helping a mage free a god from a tree. It was all too absurd to believe. She chuckled to herself. She even had a Necromancer teaching her! Maybe she was fairy folk after all.

Lost in her own thoughts, she found herself before the great Elder Tree in the center of town. She did not remember coming here, but somehow she knew this was where she needed to be.

She placed her hand against the gigantic tree once again. Much like the others, all she found was the cold bark against her palm. How could they really expect her to be able pull a god from this monstrous tree, let alone be able to place it into a consort? She was a sheepherder, how had she even gotten to this point?

It wasn't fair. She stared up and up toward the canopy then past it. Stars glittered in the clear night sky; she could see heaven itself up there. She smiled inwardly, remembering the times she would sneak out of her house back home just to stare at the stars.

The full moon lit the clearing around the great maple tree and she could see the worn-down earth around the base. How many people had placed their hand where hers was now? How many people looked at those same stars and wondered if they were on the right path?

She closed her eyes and focused again on the bark below her palm. She pictured that blue sky, just like Trust had taught her.

"The tree is alive in my hand," she whispered.

"All things are alive when in your hands."

She stumbled back at the sound of another's voice and tripped over a nearby root, startled to find she was not alone.

Stone Wolf walked to her and offered her a hand. She grasped it and let him hoist her to standing again. She smiled softly to him but did not let his hand go.

"I don't think I can fix this," she said honestly.

"You don't have to fix anything." He made no move to let go of her hand. "You just have to be who you have always been. The rest will come on its own."

For the first time since arriving here, she was calm again. He was right, after all; it was silly to put so much pressure on herself. She was still the sheepherder she had been when he'd found her. Trying to force her way through her training would lead nowhere.

She reluctantly let her hand fall from his and placed it back to the trunk of the tree. He did the same. His closeness to her was painfully obvious now.

She closed her eyes and inhaled the night smells around her. Damp leaves and smoke. She breathed deeper and could pick up his lingering scent of mint on the breeze. *The tree is alive in my hand.* She felt it then, the faint pulse of life under the surface.

Her eyes snapped open and she found Stone uncomfortably close to her. Their eyes locked and she could see colors begin to flicker around him.

"Can you feel it?" Her question was barely a whisper as she stared into his eyes, seeing waves of colors reflected there. Each one bringing its own emotion.

"I have always felt it."

A nearby door slammed open, causing them both to break eye contact. Stone took a step back, leaving her alone next to the tree.

"You should not be here alone. Please come back inside with me." He had returned to the Guardian she knew him to be. It made her a little sad to see the change in him. She was tired of pretending to not be his friend, and she just wanted to stay in this moment a little longer. She looked to the stars one last time.

"I will follow you wherever you go."

# Chapter Thirty-Six

"A festival? Is that what the villagers have been setting up?" Starlyn asked him hopefully.

"The Fall Festival, to be exact. We have one every year and I was hoping you would stay long enough to attend," Pan explained as Orion casually stood speaking with Stone Wolf quietly. The group had decided to have lunch near the center of town not far off from the great maple tree and Starlyn was grateful for the break in her daily training.

The past few days had been strenuous, and her progress seemed to slow to a sudden halt. She was frustrated, Trust was frustrated, and Pan could tell it was time for a break. She beamed at the thought of attending a festival. It had been so long since life seemed normal.

"Will there be dancing?"

"Of course, but you must promise to save a dance for me."

She did not think it possible, but her smile grew even more. Like most young girls, she had dreamed about dancing with a handsome man and just the thought of the chance to fulfill that dream overwhelmed her with excitement. The only man she had danced with was her father.

"The festival will be just what we all need, a bit of relaxation." Pan said to her while snacking on a sandwich.

"Are you gonna dance with me?" she asked Stone Wolf who stopped his conversation long enough to look at her dumbfounded.

She knew he would not, but deep down she was

disappointed when he declined. At least Pan would dance with her and she was sure Trust wouldn't allow her to be left out either.

She chewed her sandwich and mused to herself about which song she would request for her first dance. The Ballad of Ricky Robert or maybe My Lady Fair? Her thoughts were interrupted by the appearance of Trust.

"Pardon the intrusion, but I believe my student has a lesson she is late for."

She groaned loudly in mock pain.

"You truly are a professional torturer, Trust."

The town was a flurry of activity as vendors began to arrive and set up booths. What she expected to take days was ready within hours. She had never seen anything like it.

There would be feats of strength, food, dancing, and even a scavenger hunt. All followed by the ceremonial offerings to the Elders.

It was a grand set up and every person she spoke with was bubbling with excitement, making it hard for her to contain her own. The first night of the festival finally arrived and at last food and drink had begun to be passed around.

"The first nights are always the wildest during these types of events." Trust whispered into her ear

The strumming of the guitars made it hard for her to hear him. When he handed her a small bottle, she brought it to her nose and gagged.

"Rum, my dear. The finest spiced rum you will find this far inland."

She took a deep swig and choked as it burned her throat. Her mouth began to salivate and she pushed the bottle back into his hands. He laughed at her, then took his own long draught. He offered it to her again and she accepted but was not as graceful as he was when she swallowed her second gulp.

Trust pushed her closer to where the crowd was gathering for dancing. He bowed to her quickly, then disappeared amongst the people.

The music was loud and Starlyn clapped in rhythm to the beat. The rum she'd consumed had gone to her head quickly and now she was ready to dance. She stamped her foot in time with the drums and laughed as the men spun the women in the air in front of her. She loved watching a good dance and wanted to join so badly.

Stone Wolf was immovable behind her as usual. Vigilant as always despite the festivities happening around them. She sighed loudly and turned back to the crowd as the pace began to pick up. She laughed as a man tried to take her hand, only to be blocked by Stone Wolf.

"No fair! You won't dance, so why can't I?"

He shook his head stoically and she stuck her tongue out at him.

She spotted Trust making his way around the circle, weaving in and out of the crowd with an expert grace. Women flocked to him, each taking a turn being spun by his hand.

The rum had made her bold and when she saw her opening, she ran for it. Bounding into Trust's arms, he did not miss a beat as he swept her away with the crowd. She whooped loudly as he spun with her around and around. She laughed so hard her cheeks burned with pleasure. Before she realized it, another man had grabbed her arm and she went spinning with him as well.

Then another, then another, and before she knew it she was dizzy with excitement, laughing uncontrollably as she floated from partner to partner. Never had she been so happy. As the dance finally ended, she found herself in the arms of a stranger. He laughed merrily alongside her and offered her a swig from his flask. She took it greedily and wrinkled her nose at the taste—that was not rum, for sure.

The man leaned in suddenly and kissed her quick and sweet before turning away, disappearing into the crowd. She lifted her hands to her lips in surprise. Her first kiss. She glanced around and saw the crowd begin to part as Stone Wolf approached her. The villagers gave him a wide berth as he stalked toward her menacingly. Well, her fun was officially over for the night—or was it?

She smiled mischievously and darted for the crowd behind her, slipping through the villagers and drunkenly bouncing off one or two. She would not be caught so easily.

It was barely ten feet before she felt the rock-hard grip of her Guardian's hand on her arm.

"Did you really think you could run?"

She squealed drunkenly when he spun her round to face him. She fell into his arms, giggling hysterically.

"It was worth a shot…" she slurred.

"By the gods, girl, when did you drink so much?"

She was unimpressed by his sour attitude and wished Trust would come rescue her for more dancing.

"Unhand me, sir. This is a party, is it not?" She ripped her arm free from his grasp, trying to sound more mature than she felt. His eyes hardened behind his mask.

"Please. This could be my last chance," she begged, not caring how childish she sounded.

He glanced down in thought and she took the momentary distraction to flee again. Giggling, she ran back toward the dancing crowd. She turned her head to see Stone Wolf within arm's reach and she put more effort into her run.

She was not paying attention and ran right into Trust's

back. He sloshed his wine onto the woman he was speaking with and she shouted in surprise.

"Dance with me!" Starlyn nearly screamed.

His face was washed with confusion and he turned to apologize to the woman, but Starlyn grabbed his hand, forcefully pulling him into the crowd.

"Please, before he catches me!"

Trust glanced behind him to see Stone Wolf calmly walking toward them. She watched the smile break over Trust's face when he realized the game she was playing. He yelled a quick apology to the woman over his shoulder as he joined her in dashing to the dance floor.

His smile matched her own and they began to weave in and out of the crowd. They danced and dodged the Guardian every time he was close, both loving their little game of Keep Away. The music began to pick up and the dance floor became more and more crowded, forcing her in close to Trust. He protectively wrapped his arms around her and continued to move through the crowd with an easy grace. She closed her eyes and let him lead her around and around, loving every second of being so close to him.

She never realized how tall he was until now. He was nearly as tall as Stone, and his brown skin seemed to glow in the torchlight. He was a very handsome man to say the least, and she found herself almost entranced by his smile. He hugged her closer as they spun near Stone Wolf, almost as if he was worried the man would snatch her from his arms.

The song finally ended and Starlyn could not control her laughter. Stone Wolf stood and anger shone in his eyes. Perhaps it was time to end her game.

She went to thank Trust but instead of words she found herself sick instead. The rum, wine, and random alcohol she had consumed combined with the excitement of spinning and came up as she retched right on Trust's feet.

Wiping her mouth, she swayed and met his eyes. His face was a mask of irritation and she felt her cheeks go red before retching again. This time she was able to stumble away from him in time to miss his shoes, thankfully.

She stayed hunched over until there was nothing left in her stomach, and even then she continued to heave. Why had she drunk so much? Finally recovering some, she stood to find Stone Wolf waiting for her. He was the last person she wanted to confront in this state.

"Leave me be, I'm fi ... fine." She hiccupped.

He closed his eyes and shook his head.

In the blink of an eye, he had her picked up in her arms and was carrying her toward the hut she was staying in. She was going to protest, but her stomach reminded her of more important things.

When he set her down on the bed, the world around her was still spinning.

"You really should be more careful. I am not here to watch you like a child."

"Good. I don't need you."

She stood and attempted to push him out of the way; she was going to be ill again. Instead of pushing him, she only succeeded at falling into his arms once more. She looked up at him through her eyelashes, realizing she was dangerously close to him. He kept his eyes locked to hers while carefully moving a stray hair behind her ear. He seemed to lean in closer and she closed her eyes, then promptly vomited on him.

# Chapter Thirty-Seven

It was well past midday before Starlyn awoke, her head throbbing. She had never felt such pain before, even when she fell from her horse. This pain was much worse. She grasped her head in her hands, willing it to stop, but nothing helped. She moaned loudly and rolled over in bed. It was much too bright in this room.

Shoving her head under her pillow, she tried again to make the headache go away. She would do anything at this point just to feel better. The sudden smell of food from outside made her stomach flip over. She held back the urge to vomit again. Why did people drink when this was the result? It was torture.

She rolled in bed for a long time before there was a knock at the door. She tried to ignore it, knowing answering it would mean facing the world when she felt like dying instead. There was another more insistent knock, and it was obvious she couldn't avoid it any longer.

"Yes?" She flinched at her own snippy tone.

The door creaked open a crack and Dove peered in. When she saw Starlyn on the bed, she opened the door the rest of the way.

"Good day, love. You cannot stay in bed *all* day," she berated her playfully. "You will miss the feats of strength!"

Starlyn moaned in response. The last thing she cared about was watching men show off how strong they were.

Dove ignored her protest and began filling a basin with water. She then came over and with a jerk, stole the blanket from the bed, leaving Starlyn to hide under her pillow.

"Don't make me take ya pillow away too, milady."

She moaned but finally yielded, making her way to the

basin. With a whoosh of cold water, she splashed her face. It was the coldest water she had ever used.

"You could have warned me," she sputtered.

"And miss the look on ya face? No, I think not." Dove chuckled in return. "Ya don't drink much, do ya, love? Well, it may be a few hours before you start feeling better, but by tomorrow you'll feel right as rain."

Tomorrow? She would have to deal with this until tomorrow? She groaned again and flopped back onto the bed.

"Now that's enough of that, girl. It's well past time to be dressed. That Guardian of yours has been pacing outside all morning."

She popped her head up from the pillow. Hadn't something happened with him last night? *Oh my gods.* She pictured herself getting sick down the front of him. Oh no, no, no. She could not face him.

"I think I'm too sick to leave my room today."

Dove harrumphed at that but did not protest any further.

"Well, let me get ya some food, then."

The idea of food made her stomach do flips. She did not think she could muster the courage to try and eat anything at the moment but she wanted Dove to leave her alone, so she didn't argue with her. She left finally after laying out some clothes for Starlyn.

She dressed quickly even though she did not want to, but she was glad she did when there was another knock on the door. Not waiting for her permission, in walked Trust followed closely by Stone Wolf. Her face burned at the sight of them.

"So how is the life of the party doing today?"

Trust smiled wickedly at his own joke and she turned her eyes away from his.

"I'm sorry for my behavior ... to both of you." She knew her ears were redder than a tomato, and she did not dare look at either of them as she spoke. "I don't drink very often."

"I have never heard a truer statement, my dear. I must say

it was quite entertaining to watch you try to outrun a Guardian Elite."

Again, her face flushed crimson, suddenly remembering herself doing exactly what Trust said. She put her face in her hands.

"Do not be embarrassed, girl. We've all had a time or two while drinking that we would like to forget. I had to give you some grief, as you ruined my boots." He chuckled merrily but his reassurances did not help her sense of pride.

She glanced up to Stone Wolf and found him silent as usual. He refused to meet her eye. Disappointment washed over her, and she hoped he wasn't too angry with her.

"Pan would like to see you once you have recovered," Stone said, shocking both Trust and herself.

"Oh gods, did I throw up on him too?'

After Dove returned with the food, Starlyn found herself surprisingly hungry. She wasn't hopeful that she would be able to keep it down, yet she somehow had managed it. Trust had pilfered some coffea for her as well and she couldn't be more grateful to him. She chatted with Trust for some time as Stone Wolf stood silent next to the door. They both ignored him since it seemed this was going to be his current mood for the day.

It wasn't long after they ate when another knock at the door came and Pan was let into the room. Starlyn was getting tired again, but she knew she would have to make time for the Elder's mage.

"I was hoping you would allow me to escort you around the festival booths today?"

She smiled politely in return even though a walk was the last thing she wanted to do. "Of course!"

The two of them, accompanied by Trust and their Guardians, left to explore the grounds. They wandered for a time, admiring a large variety of jewelry and clothing. There were exotic rugs from the south along with incense and spices. She took it all in hungrily, as it was the first time she'd seen anything so tantalizing.

Her gaze swept the stalls with a greedy fascination until she felt someone's eyes on her. Glancing up, she did not see anyone in her immediate party watching her, yet the feeling was still there.

She had learned to trust her instincts and began scanning the crowd discreetly, which was when she locked eyes with a woman with bright blonde hair. She would know those stunning ice blue eyes anywhere and she took a few steps back, realizing the woman was actually here and not in her dreams.

Pan noticed her as well and stiffened slightly. He turned to Starlyn. "I am running out of time—there are things you must know about the Elders still." His sudden change of subject caught her attention. "That is really why I wanted to walk with you today."

He placed his hand on her back, motioning her to continue walking, and he left it there as he lowered his voice. "You must be careful with the ones who live in that mountain. There is a reason I do not stay there anymore. Those Elders and I had a falling out, you could say." He drifted off again, appearing to remember something that she could not begin to grasp. "Do not trust them, their intentions may not b—"

He inhaled sharply.

Starlyn stopped walking as the arm on her shoulder became heavy. Pan's face was contorted in pain. Only then did she see the man had a sword protruding from his chest.

Fear gripped her and she stepped back as he slumped to the ground. Orion stood behind him, bloody sword in hand. His eyes focused on her with determination. Pan's body lay on the ground, his blood pooling around her slippers.

Starlyn knew that she should move, that she should step away from the blood and go back to her room, run and hide. She knew she should do something—anything. But she couldn't make herself move. She stared at the red stain that began to soak into her slippers. Vaguely she knew people around her were screaming, vaguely she knew they were running, and yet the world seemed unimportant to her.

The blonde woman smiled at her now as villagers ran around her in a panic. A single sound broke through to Starlyn's ears, a sound that made her skin crawl and her mind focus immediately. It was the loud howl breaking through the commotion that finally made her run.

# Chapter Thirty-Eight

Stone Wolf watched Starlyn and Pan talk out of the corner of his eye. He did not want to take his eyes off her for long; he had no idea how long her strength would hold up after her night of overindulgence. Orion was unusually silent today and that also put him on edge for some reason. His fellow *Beschermer* was usually more upbeat. Something was happening here and he wanted to be ready for anything.

They had spent a long time walking in and out of the many stalls set up for the festival. He could hear their casual conversations as they discussed each interesting ware they found. It all felt very normal, yet the hair on his neck was standing on end.

He surveyed the crowd, but nothing seemed out of the ordinary. Villagers surrounded them, laughing and talking amongst themselves. Children ran between stalls playing games of tag. It was just as it should be.

The wind shifted, now blowing from behind him, and with it came the sudden images of wolves in the woods. He breathed deep, trying to interpret the pictures. The pack was near, very near. He took a second and glanced over his shoulder, hoping he was wrong. At that moment, his sensitive ears picked up the soft hiss of a sword being drawn.

He glanced back just in time to see Orion ram his blade into Pan's back. Without thinking, Stone Wolf drew his own sword, and at the same moment the town erupted with motion. Screams echoed through the trees, followed by a now familiar howl. The pack had arrived.

He turned at the heavy thud of footsteps behind him, just in time to roll out of the path of a Night Runner. In the same motion, he grabbed the hatchet strapped to his thigh and hurled it toward the animal. The weapon stuck in the beast's shoulder blade, causing it to stumble to the ground and effectively distracting it from Starlyn, who now was running toward the trees.

The Night Runner howled as it turned toward Stone and began to circle him. Stone Wolf quickly took in his surroundings. This had to be over quick; Starlyn was alone. Before he had a chance to make his move, Trust was at his side.

"Go, I can handle this one," he said, his sword already drawn.

Stone Wolf leapt in action, following Starlyn's trail into the surrounding woods.

It didn't take long for him to catch up with her, and judging by the sounds of cracking branches surrounding them he was not the only one that followed her. He watched as she tripped over a fallen tree and began to crawl her way forward. He easily scooped her up and continued running despite her screams. He nearly dropped her once as she struggled against his hold, fighting with all she had.

"ENOUGH!" he bellowed.

Realization finally dawned on her and she stopped kicking, then clung to him tightly.

"Pan is not dead. You can still save him." He spoke while running and she bounced in his arms as he leaped over a fallen tree.

"How?" she asked.

"If you free the Elder from the tree, you can save them both."

She chewed on her lower lip. He knew she could do it, he

just hoped she would agree. Finally, he saw resolve take shape in her eyes and he knew she had made her decision

"Take me back."

Starlyn raced toward the center of town. The village was full of cries for help and at least one building had been set aflame. How had so much damage been dealt in such a small time? She had to get to the Elder Tree.

Stone jogged beside her, pushing people out of her way with ease. He dispatched a random attacker as they moved in but kept her moving forward. At last, she found herself standing in front of the giant maple. As she went to put her hand on the trunk, a gigantic man stepped in front of her, blocking her path.

His eyes were bright red and he was covered in flowing tattoos. He stood shirtless and sneered at her, showing sharp teeth behind his smile. She had never seen such a terrifying person before in her life. Who was he?

Stone Wolf pushed her behind him, shielding her from the monster's view.

"I will have the bitch," the newcomer growled out low and menacingly.

She stiffened at the harshness of the statement and took a step back. Stone wolf glanced back, making sure she was far enough away to not be hurt, and drew the blade he kept on his back. The cold enveloped her and frosted over the clearing surrounding the Elder Tree.

The other man did not flinch at the change in temperature and a half smile reached his lips.

"It will take more than the cold to stop me from killing the wench."

Starlyn began to tremble. Was it from the cold or from fear?

"Free the Elder, save Pan!" Stone said over his shoulder, bringing her attention back to the task at hand.

He lunged forward. To her shock, the unarmed man easily dodged the blade and jumped atop Stone Wolf. A guttural snarl escaped from Stone's lips as he hit the ground hard, sword falling from his grasp. A distant howl shook her to her core ... The tree, get to the tree.

She ran to the Elder Tree, not knowing how she was going to pull this off. Fear coursed through her whole body as she placed both palms to the tree. *Blue sky, blue sky, blue sky.* She tried to concentrate but was interrupted by a crash behind her. Two monstrous wolves crouched where the men had once been. The red-eyed wolf was horrifying with his white fur swirled with black, matching his tattoos from his human form. He dwarfed Stone Wolf, and she began to sweat. *Focus,* she reminded herself.

She turned to the tree and tried again.

"The tree is alive in my hand," she whispered, but nothing happened.

*Damn it.* Why wasn't it working? She closed her eyes, drowning out the world around her. *The tree is alive in my hand ... The tree is alive ... The tree. No.* It suddenly made sense to her. The tree was not alive—the *man* was alive in the tree.

She thought back to the night her and Stone spent here. What had he told her? All things were alive in her hands? She hurriedly put her hands back on the trunk.

"The *man* is alive in my hands, the man is alive," she said under her breath.

There it was, the heartbeat she knew would be there. She focused on the beating rhythm and the pulse in her hands. *The man is alive in my hands.* She carefully wrapped her mind around that heartbeat, ever so gently cradling it.

Last time she had tried to force it out, had tried to pull it to her, but this time would be different. She did not need to force anything, she just needed to ask. She reached deep within the heartbeat and began to coax it closer to the surface. Slowly, it became stronger, until she could actually hear it beating.

The battle between wolves raged on behind her and pushed the sounds away. They were just clouds and she needed her blue sky.

"Come home. It's time to come home."

She pressed her cheek to the tree and the world burst into color. It radiated from everything but the tree seemed to be the brightest. It was like the sun shone from its bark. She welcomed it with an open heart and envisioned Pan joining with the light. She pictured his smile and kind words. Pictured that sunshine filling him and his wounds knitting together.

When the connection finally became complete, she sucked in a sharp breath. She was going to faint. She wavered from the tree, feeling utterly sick. As she reeled and fell back against the giant tree, she thought she saw something in the clearing by her.

It was a woman. Her blonde hair shone in the sunlight and her icy blue eyes bore into her almost painfully. She smiled at Starlyn and held out her hand. In her palm lay a four-leaf clover.

Stone watched Starlyn stumble and knew it was time to leave. He would not allow her to be hurt. Gibbous was a fierce fighter, but he was losing energy quickly. He wasn't far from *Hemel Deur*. If he could get the girl there, she would be safe.

He easily shifted into his human form and scooped up Niets from where it had fallen. He turned to swing at Gibbous and found he had shifted as well. Blood ran down his chest from the wounds Stone had inflicted. Without thinking, he threw the remaining knives from his arm at the man and they embedded in his chest. Gibbous roared in frustration and swiped the blades from his body.

Stone used the distraction to throw Starlyn over his shoulder. The alpha may be weakened but Stone Wolf was at a disadvantage by carrying the girl. He had to rely on every bit of strength he had left. He had to outrun the man, he *had* to get Starlyn to safety.

He ran at full speed away from the clearing and headed into the woods toward *Hemel Deur*. All around him was chaos as the pack tore through the village. He ignored them all and ran on. If he lost focus for even one second, he would lose his advantage.

He could hear the pack closing in behind them and he pushed himself harder. Blood-streaked sweat rolled down his mask into his eyes as he ran. His clothes were in tatters and most of his weapons were gone. He could not falter, not with so much to lose.

They would not have her; he would not let them touch her. With the last of his energy, he put more effort into running. *I must protect her.*

He easily dodged branches and jumped over fallen trees in his path as he ran even faster, the pack on his heels. His legs were on fire from the exertion but he would not slow down. The trail he followed began to widen and he knew it wouldn't be much further now. *Just keep moving.*

The trees around him seemed to erupt with motion. The familiar uniforms of *De Zoekers* of *Hemel Deur* burst from the trees but he did not slow. He rounded the bend and was never happier to see the giant iron door standing open.

At least a half dozen Keepers waited for him and several *Beschermer* joined while he ran through the door. He did not come to a stop until he was well inside the fortress and he knew Starlyn would be safe at last.

Thank you for reading!

I hope you enjoyed the book as much as I enjoyed writing it.

If you could spare two minutes of your time to write a review,

I would be really grateful and very happy to read it!

Please review on Amazon.com or Goodreads.com today.

Thank you

Crystal Matthews

www.crystalmatthews.net

# About The Author

## Crystal Matthews

 Crystal was born in eastern Washington where she was found by fairies under a rock amongst the sage brush.

She was raised by wolves in the North Cascades and it was here she developed a strong love for nature and the mountains.

Rain makes her smile and sunshine gives her strength. She is friends with the moon and knows, when the time comes, she will meet with her loved ones at the North Star. Her personality is her super power.

Basically, Crystal loves to read, create, all thing Fantasy and anything that has to do with being outside

# Books In This Series

*Legend of the Dawn Child*

**Burdens Of Blood**

**Betrayal Of Blood**

Made in the USA
Columbia, SC
12 October 2024

44233189R00150